Naperville, Chicag

An Exploration into Naperville's Bizarre History
and True Stories of its Unrested Dead

3rd Edition
Kevin J. Frantz

To [an old friend]
ain't
I just dug up...
2015

HauntedNaperville.com

Naperville, Chicago's Haunted Neighbor 3rd Edition © 2013 by Kevin J. Frantz. All rights reserved. No part of this book may be used, transmitted, or reproduced in any manner whatsoever, including live performance, Internet usage, without written permission from the author, except in the case of quotations embodied in critical articles, stories, and reviews.

Book cover design by Kevin Frantz
Photo of Kevin on back cover by Elise Frantz
Edited by Janice Sanders
Published by Unrested Dead Publishing

Special thanks go out to the Naperville Library, Evergreen Park Library, Diane Ladley, Alexander Felix, Chuck Kennedy, Curt Morley, Beth Shields, Kirsten Tillman, The Paranormal Cops Team, Scott MacKay, Denise Crosby, my beautiful wife Janice, and my unbelievable kids Jacob & Elise.

Printed in the United States of America

Visit Kevin online:
The Official Ghost Tours of Naperville – **HauntedNaperville.com**

Kevin can be contacted at (630) 205-2664. Or by email at: Info@HauntedNaperville.com

Naperville, Chicago's Haunted Neighbor

An Exploration into Naperville's Bizarre History
and True Stories of its Unrested Dead

3rd Edition

Kevin J. Frantz

HauntedNaperville.com

A Poem from a Naperville newspaper –

The DuPage County Observer

October 1853

Can the Spirit Die?

By C. D. Stuart

When the spirit is quenched by the finger of death,

And the lamp that enshrined it is cold,

Does the flame that illumined it die with the breath,

And mingle and pass with the mold?

Are the thoughts of the mind and the hopes of the heart

As brittle and brief as the clay,

That is born with the breath, and dies with the breath,

And is lost in the lap of decay?

Oh, no ! when the lamp shall be shiver'd in dust,

The Spirit that kindled its light

Will rise and expand with a mightier glow,

And sparkle eternally bright!

Every thought of the mind, every hope of the heart

Surviving, shall conquer in death;

'Tis the lamp that is frail, 'tis the body shall fail,

Not the soul-light that mocks at a breath.

HauntedNaperville.com

Table of Contents

Introduction – Pg. 11
   That Night in the Cemetery Changed Everything – Pg. 13
   Don't Pick Up Hitch-Hiking Ghosts – Pg. 17
A Quick Naperville History – Pg. 21
Naperville's First Ghostly Encounter – Pg. 29
The Haunted Theater – Pg. 31
   A Hollywood Honey – Pg. 34
   Playing it Safe – Pg. 38
Ace Keller – Pg. 43
The Prestidigitation of The Mysterious Smith – Pg. 45
I Want to Be a Fireman – Pg. 49
Movie and a Murder – Pg. 55
The Naperville Phantom – Pg. 63
   He's Been Seen Outside – Pg. 65
   He's Been Seen Inside – Pg. 66
   He's In Every Corner of Naperville – Pg. 68
   He Haunts Central Park – Pg. 71
   It's Not Pretty, But Here's the Truth... – Pg. 73
   It's Showtime... – Pg. 77
   Blood Money – Pg. 81
   The Plot Thickens – Pg. 85
   Tying It Together – Pg. 89
   The Sts. Peter and Paul Fire – Pg. 93
Calling Dr. Ghostly – Pg. 99
A Murderer Amongst Us – Pg. 107
Haunted Horse Clops – Pg. 109
Little Girl Lost – Pg. 113
The Flower of Fort Hill – Pg. 115

Table of Contents (continued)

Ffeiffer Hall's Second-Act Sally – Pg. 123
Upstairs / Downstairs – Pg. 131
Step Right Up – Pg. 133
Coffins, Coffins, Everywhere – Pg. 137
April 25th, 1946 - 1:03pm – Pg. 143
The Little Boy Who Sings Down the Lane – Pg. 145
He Sits on Your Bed – Pg. 147
The Whole Tooth – Pg. 151
The Secret of Heatherton Hall – Pg. 153
Happy Birthday to Me – Pg. 159
Victorian Naperville and Pre-mature Burial – Pg. 161
Riding Off Into the Sunset – Pg. 165
Fright Night – Pg. 171
    I'm Talking to the Old Lady – Pg. 175
    A Whistle From Another Time – Pg. 177
    The Crosses Crashed – Pg. 181
    Creepy Creak – Pg. 183
    Are You There, Gladys? – Pg. 185
Naperville's Wicked Witch – Pg. 187
Burying Naperville's Dead – Pg. 193
    Naperville's Undertakers – Pg. 195
    Coffins, and Preparing the Dead… - Pg. 203
    Tombstones and Flowers – Pg. 209
    Naperville's Cemeteries – Pg. 211
Naperville's First Halloween Party? – Pg. 217
    The Witches Waddle – Pg. 219
Closing Words

HauntedNaperville.com

A few words about this new edition

I could have never imagined the positive response I have received from this book – not just from Napervillians, but people all over America who have purchased it online. And while I appreciate all the nice emails I receive, I can't take all the credit - Naperville's ghostly history is so rich the book practically writes itself!

In addition, because of this book's popularity, my tours have exploded in attendance as enthusiasts from all over, travel to Naperville to have me personally regale them with Naperville's unrivaled tales of the its unrested dead. To all of you I have to say, "Thank you so very much for supporting my tour!"

Some of the stories from previous editions of this book have been updated with new data for this new edition. As well, some of the "fan favorite" stories that I've told on my tour are included herein - among them such tantalizing tales as: The Naperville Phantom, He Sits on Your Bed, Haunted Horse Clops, and Naperville's Wicked Witch.

I must point out that there is one Naperville tale from my tour that I had originally intended to include in this new edition, but, as I began to lay it out for the book, it became painfully clear to me that the story was waaaay too big to be a part of a collection of stories - it deserved its own treatment - that is the story of Naperville's Grave Robber. So, I'm happy to report, it did get its own book! My new book, currently available everywhere, is called: The Grave Robber Next Door... A Love Story. It tells (for the first time ever) the true story behind Naperville's infamous grave robber. And what a tale it is!

I wrote the book, but it wouldn't have been possible without the research assistance of my investigation partner Chuck Kennedy. Without him the truth behind Naperville's grave robber would have never been so completely and thoroughly told. Thanks Chuck!

May you enjoy these new books as much as I enjoyed producing them.

Kev

2013

Introduction

I grew up in the 1960s & 70s. While my peers watched The Brady Bunch and Hogan's Heroes, I was fascinated by Twilight Zone, One Step Beyond, and Night Gallery; is it any wonder I should be sitting here 35 years later relaying stories of unrested dead? Is it simply my destiny catching up with me? I do have to admit that I find the dead overtly interesting – more interesting in fact than those who actually *breathe*.

You and I are probably much alike in that respect.

People have asked me, "Doesn't researching death get a little depressing?" On the contrary, when I bury my face in history, I avoid the tumultuously depressing headlines of today. I think I'm getting a decent deal.

It has always been my desire to answer bigger-than-life questions. This desire, at age 30, lead me to secure a Bachelor of Arts in Biblical Study degree, thinking that perhaps the ministry was my calling. Alas, I was soon turned off by the politics and business of it all and gave up in disgust. "God knows where to find me," I thought. Of course, I didn't abandon *God*, just the system. (I can't help but feel that God is probably disgusted by the politics and business of it all as well). Christian beliefs are still very much a part of me. I'm sure they guide me and protect me much more than I'll ever understand while walking Earth.

I grew up in the south Chicago suburb of Evergreen Park, graduating from Evergreen Park High School in 1978. I played bass in rock bands and was infected by the dream of rock stardom. Because of this, I delayed college and entered the workforce in a new field called "Video." VHS videotape and VCR's were an unbelievable technology in 1980, and I soon found myself immersed in it.

In 1982, I started a video business that converted old home-movie films to VHS. That business, though ahead of its time, was doing very well. I soon partnered with my brother, John. We opened two videotape rental stores. They, too, did remarkably well. At the age of 24, I was the employer of about 30 people.

By 1986, I was also videotaping weddings and building an arsenal of video recording gear - gear that 16 years later would open the door to paranormal investigation and recording.

I sold my video rental businesses in the late 1980s and moved to Naperville in 1992, bringing with me my video production business. I set up as Memories Productions. (MemoriesRescued.com)

At this point I began dabbling in a love of my childhood - ghostly fiction. My writing, called "The Journals of Father Nick Thomas," became very popular online and went on to win an Internet award. At that time I began to train in the arena of public speaking. It soon earned me the coveted "Speaker of the Year" award from a regional division of the Toastmasters Speaking Organization. These awards planted in me the confidence to begin producing material and presenting publicly. The problem was that I didn't know *what* to present.

Several years passed and then one day, while surfing the internet, I saw a teaser headline that read: "Do You Have What It Takes to Be a Ghost Hunter?" "Ghost hunting?" I thought, "Sounds interesting..." I clicked the headline and was taken to a story about the process of ghost hunting. Basically, the article concluded that all a would-be ghost hunter needed - in order to get started in ghost hunting - was patience, nerve, and the right type of video camcorder (which, as it turns out, I had from my video recording business). I called my wife, Janice, and suggested that we go ghost hunting that night.

She enthusiastically agreed.

We decided to go to the Naperville Cemetery on Washington Street for our first foray into the unknown world of ghost hunting. We couldn't wait for dark...

That Night in the Cemetery Changed Everything...

We would be using a standard camcorder, but we'd be recording in the dark using invisible infrared light. Without getting technical, infrared light allows us to record in total darkness because infrared light illuminates the area for the recorder, but the light is not visible to our eyes. If a paranormal situation occurs, the paranormal matter (or energy) will reflect the infrared light back toward the camera, in essence "painting" a picture of the ghostly image on the recording – even though the ghostly image is invisible! *This is so cool.*

The time was approximately 10p.m., mid-July 2002. Armed in the pitch dark with a video camera I'd held a thousand times before, I felt a new found exhilaration as I cradled it in my palm. The words of the story I'd read were echoing in my head, "Many people with basic infrared photography gear are capturing paranormal images that can't be explained away easily." I remember thinking, "I could actually record a ghost here tonight!" My heart raced. I admit I was a little bit scared. But I stared off into the darkness of the cemetery, daring it to stop me. I turned to my wife, "It's time." I turned on the power to the camera, engaged the infrared light, and we slid through the fence.

(Teachable moment here - I was an ultra-novice-ghost-hunter at this time. I have since learned that a responsible ghost hunter NEVER trespasses on private property, ever. Get permission or don't go. There are no exceptions to this rule).

The remote area of the cemetery was pitch dark. The disruption of the grass as we walked through it caused the insects of mid-July in Illinois to be stirred up. In short, we were being eaten alive. I resisted the urge to flee, concluding that *something or someone wanted us to leave*. For that reason alone I was determined to stay.

Only a few more moments of torture in the darkness continued before the screen of my video camcorder flashed brightly. It appeared, in the camera screen, to be a large ball of light with a tail. It seemed to fly right in front of me, about knee level. It flew left to right, and continued around behind me. It stopped me in my tracks, as I frantically looked behind me to see if I could see it with my naked eye... Nope, just dark. And lots of it.

I stood in the stillness of the dark cemetery. A mosquito screeched in my ear and I swatted it away. "*Something is here,*" I whispered to no one. I just saw it on the camera's screen. *I know* it's here. Where is it now? I waited, moving not a muscle. Is it coming back?

After a moment I called to my wife, "Janice, I think we got something, the screen just lit up like a splitting atom." We quickly made our way out to the street - away from the insects that were having us for dinner. There we reviewed the tape. A still frame from the video is below.

In this still frame image, you can see the bright head of the anomaly and its tail. It is about 12 feet long.

The next day was a new day for me. I was now on a quest. I'd had my first paranormal encounter and there was just one thing to say: I wanted another one.

That experience in the darkened cemetery changed the direction of my life. I began to learn all I could about the process of ghost hunting. As I learned, I taught others. I started, and served as president of, the Heartland

Paranormal Research and Education Society. In addition, I have been interviewed dozens of times as a ghost hunting authority for radio and print relating to ghosts and research.

Over the years, I have participated in dozens of investigations with many incredible results. There was the investigation of the Four Mounds Mansion in Iowa in which the deceased owner of the mansion, an elderly Victorian woman who has been haunting the structure for decades, disapproved of my wife and I sleeping in her room. She did so by telling me "I was an intruder" and to "get out of her home." When I shared this story with two of the psychics who have communicated many times with the old woman, they told me that she always refers to both of them as "uninvited intruders."

There was also the time in Alton, Illinois, when I picked up a hitch-hiking ghost...

HauntedNaperville.com

Don't Pick Up Hitch-Hiking Ghosts...

My wife and I decided to spend a weekend in haunted Alton in a haunted cottage - The Doyle Cottage. We'd spent Saturday night on a personal ghost tour of the city with a talented tour guide named Antoinette. We retired late that night.

On Sunday morning we awoke early, had breakfast and headed out to revisit some of the haunted sites from last night - this time on our own. It was about 2 p.m. when we headed into the Alton Cemetery.

The Alton Cemetery is a pre-Civil War cemetery on a large hill. As you scale the 20 or so steps to the top, the cemetery itself is above you and hidden. It's not until you reach the top steps that the vast acreage of ancient trees and stones unfold before you like an opening coffin - slightly unnerving.

As we continued walking through the cemetery, we spotted an old woman sitting on a tombstone about 30 feet ahead of us. She was watching us as we drew closer to her. She appeared to be homeless, as her features were quite worn and weathered and her clothing shabby. She had next to her a carpetbag. As we passed her she whispered, "Excuse me..."

We stopped and turned our attention to her. I assumed she'd be asking for money - I was wrong. She quickly asked, "Could you give me a ride?" Trying to find a way out of the situation, I blurted, "We're not from around here."

She interjected with, "just to the women's shelter, it's near the casino..." I knew where the casino was, but I delayed the answer by telling her that my wife and I would talk about it. She sensed that I was blowing her off; I could see that she was disappointed.

My wife and I continued walking a few moments then stopped. I looked back and the woman was still sitting on the tombstone about 150 feet away from us. My wife thought that I should give the woman a ride. I asked, "What if she tries to kill me?" I didn't know her; she could be desperate and dangerous.

My wife convinced me to do it by suggesting that she wait in the cemetery for my return. That way, if the woman tried anything with me, my wife would know whom I was with. It seemed like a plan.

We went back to the woman, and I agreed to drive her. My wife stayed behind.

The woman and I got in my car and proceeded down a short road toward the river; I knew the casino was along the river not far from where we were. After a moment the woman asked, "What were you doing in the cemetery?" I responded that we were ghost hunters and were taking pictures. She asked, "Have you ever seen a ghost?" I said, "Yes." She asked, "How do you know I'm not a ghost?" I was taken back by the question, but she looked very serious. I responded, "I guess I don't..." She nodded and turned, looking out her window.

After a moment she asked - while continuing to look out the window – "How do you know I'm not going to kill you?" That freaked me out! That's what I'd asked my wife 10 minutes earlier, and there is no way this woman could have heard it! I jokingly answered, "I guess I don't. But if you do, at least I was doing something nice when it happened!" She didn't respond.

A moment later she pointed to an empty parking lot and said, "Let me out here, in there." I pulled into the middle of the lot and got out to open her door for her. We walked around to the driver's side door, where she said, "Thank you. It was very nice of you to help me. Do you always help people?" I shrugged my shoulders, confessing, "I can't change the world, but if I can help someone, I'll try." She said, "Thanks." I turned and opened the car door and then turned back to say good-bye. But, she was gone! There was nowhere for her to go! She was old and carrying her large carpet bag besides!

I quickly ran to the street to see if, by some freak of physics, she had gotten that far away in two seconds. She wasn't there. She had vanished as soon as I turned my back to open the car door!

When I returned to the cemetery, my wife saw me come over the hill and shouted to me sarcastically, "I'm glad you made it back in one piece!" I yelled, "You aren't going to believe this..."

As my experiences grew, I spoke to more and more people about ghosts. Ghost stories of Naperville began to literally come out of the woodwork. Ghosts and Naperville seemed to have an intimate relationship - more so than other towns seemed to experience. I began to chronicle the stories, and on occasion, formally investigate them. These stories led to my live Ghost Tour of Naperville being produced. (HauntedNaperville.com)

I personally lead the tours on the pitch-dark streets of haunted Naperville. Few experiences are as exhilarating as relating true stories of Naperville's ghosts to wide-eyed participants on the tours.

As so many Naperville ghost stories continue to be shared with me, I have found it necessary to chronicle them in book form. In the beginning I felt that the live tour would suffice, but it is getting to a point that the stories will be lost to the ages if we don't start getting them in print. A wise person once said, "The greatest mind is weaker than the palest ink."

I receive calls and emails almost daily from Naperville residents with a story or experience to share. I encourage anyone with a "Naperville ghostly encounter tale" to call or email me. We are making an effort to preserve these experiences for future generations; please don't take a piece of Naperville's history with you when you go! (I am often asked if real names are used in the stories. No, they are not. Actual names are confidential, and in many cases unknown even to me).

Most of what you'll read here is brand new information. I will attempt to separate old Naperville folklore tales from those tales with historical evidence and/or firsthand eyewitness evidence. This is the first time most of these subjects are being discussed publicly, especially the true story of Naperville's Phantom.

I do try to back up theories put forth with historical background. Please note however that in the course of my research for this work it was not unusual for dates or descriptions to be at odds in the historical records. I have labored to be as factual as possible, often having to choose the most feasible information between opposing accounts of the same event. If you feel there is a factual error, by all means kindly email with the details. I will look into the matter further for a possible correction in future editions of this work.

The true stories in this volume come from my personal experiences, newspaper accounts, local folklore, police reports, and personal interviews with the participants. Names have been changed unless otherwise stated.

I have elected also to keep residential addresses private in order not to infringe on the privacy of individuals. Public buildings will have their actual addresses disclosed.

The stories in this book are intermingled and fall into one of two themes. They are:

1) **Naperville Ghosts**. These are true stories of ghostly encounters within the city of Naperville, IL

2) **The Streets of Naperville**. These are strange and bizarre events that have unfolded on the streets of Naperville.

Enjoy,

Kevin Frantz, 2012

HauntedNaperville.com

A Quick Naperville History

First of all, Naperville is an amazing city. All its prestigious awards are too numerous to list...

A few:

* #1 place to raise a family

* #1 place to start a home-based business

* Two of the top 5 school districts in the nation

* Highest standard of living in the nation

* Second largest Chamber of commerce in the state of Illinois, only Chicago's Chamber is larger

* #1 Illinois festival (The Exchange Club's annual Ribfest)

* #1 Library system in the nation, 8 years in a row

* One of the fastest growing cities in the nation

* Award-winning college radio station

* Most family-friendly town in America

* Dozens of athletic and media awards for the high schools & college

And if those accolades weren't enough –

* Adolph Coors, founder of the Coors Beer Brewing Company, learned to brew beer in Naperville.

* Ray Kroc, founder of McDonald's Restaurants, learned the fast food business while working for Cock Robin restaurants, based in Naperville.

* A Naperville resident, Jim "Soni" Sonefeld, is the drummer for music

supergroup Hootie and the Blowfish.

* Paula Zahn, news anchor/TV personality, is a native Napervillian.

* A Naperville resident invented the wireless TV remote control!

* Gena Glockson, a Naperville resident, made it into American Idol's top 10 in 2006.

* Dick Locher, who has drawn the Dick Tracy comic strip for a quarter century, has lived in Naperville for 40 years.

And these are just a few examples.

The seeds for this greatness were planted long ago...

The founder of Naperville, Joseph Naper, was born in Bennington, Virginia. At a young age he moved with his brothers, sisters and parents to Ohio. Joe visited this area in February of 1831 and wanted to make it his home. He returned to Ohio to settle affairs. Then on July 15, 1831, Joe Naper sold his brother Benjamin's boat for him to a buyer in Chicago. Joe then delivered the boat – named The Telegraph – by sailing it to Chicago from Ohio.

Joe Naper, and several other families with him, set out to settle their homesteads. They built their crude huts on a piece of ground that is today approximately at the spot where Ogden Avenue intersects Columbia Street (1/2 mile east of Washington Street.)

Contrary to popular belief, Joe Naper and his fellow pioneers were not the first non-Indians here. When they arrived, the Scott family and Hobson's were already settled – and the area was referred to as Scott's Settlement. The Scott family had originally come from Maryland. At first they settled in what is now Evanston, Illinois, but on a hunting trip they discovered this area and moved here.

At the time, the area was also popular to Native American Indians. In fact, there have been artifacts unearthed along the DuPage River that suggest more than 30 separate tribes have lived along the river that runs through the ground that would eventually become Naperville.

The grounds were very fertile, both in plant and animal. But it was also a very dangerous place. The early settlers in this area never knew when a marauding Indian might jump out of the darkness, grab them by the hair and proceed to remove their head. There were constant dangers. Still they remained firm.

In May of 1832 there were about 200 settlers in the settlement. It was at that time that a Potawatomi Indian named Shattee, who was friendly with the settlers, was asked to help kill the settlers by the Black Hawk Indians. Shattee informed the settlers of the Black Hawk plan. The story is that the women and children were quickly moved to Fort Dearborn in Chicago. It was a two-day journey from Naperville. (Its location was where Michigan Avenue passes over the Chicago River). But their quick relocation isn't exactly the truth...

It seems Joe Naper may have been a mystic of-sorts. He had befriended an old Indian medicine woman, who apparently would give him advice that he followed stubbornly. During the Black Hawk War preparations, Joe Naper wasn't all that keen on leaving the settlement because of the advice he was getting from the woman. He changed his mind, however, only when the old medicine woman finally told him "It is time." It was then that he began evacuating the women and children to Chicago.

The men then began building a fort that they could use for protection while defending their homesteads. It was called Fort Payne, and it was built on the hill where today Chicago Avenue and Ellsworth Street intersect, south side. There is a ¼ size replica of it in the Naper Settlement Museum. Thankfully, before they finished building the fort, a treaty was signed, peace was restored, and the women and children returned.

(There was a widely popular story that Indians killed Joe Naper and his family after returning from Fort Dearborn, but that he first killed nine

Indians himself! This is not true; Joe Naper returned to Naperville peacefully. He died in his sleep from a heart condition on August 24, 1862).

With the Black Hawk War behind them, Joe Naper began to take the initiative to build commerce in the area, organize small governmental bodies, establish churches, schools, streets, laws, etc. Soon people began referring to the area as Naper's Settlement (evidentially the Scott's didn't care.) The area, under Joe Naper's leadership, began to grow and prosper.

Naper's Settlement was incorporated as a city in 1861 and officially became the "City of Naperville." Interestingly, Joe Naper didn't want to name the town "Naperville." He wanted to call it simply "Naper." He was outvoted.

One of our early crown jewels was the Pre-emption House. It was built in 1834 on the southeast corner of Jackson and Main Street (The spot is currently occupied by Sullivan's restaurant.) The Pre-emption House was razed in 1946.

The Pre-emption House got its name from the Pre-Emption Act of 1841. This act of Congress gave American settlers the right to claim up to 160 acres of unclaimed land, paying the government just $1.60 an acre. The paperwork and payments for land claims in this area were transacted within the Pre-Emption House walls.

The Pre-emption House was also a hotel. It was a beautiful structure; constructed of locally grown oak and walnut - all the trim was white pine, floors were maple. Because of its professionalism and comfort, the Pre-emption House Hotel attracted many influential people through its doors. It was an all-in-one business center, tavern, hotel, stable, restaurant, and fun place. It had over 30 furnished sleeping rooms, stables for over 50 horses, and storage for carriages and buggies. The housekeepers there were paid $8 a week, a lot of money for the time. It was comfortable and a bargain too - you could have your horse fed and boarded overnight, as well as have a fresh supper, spend the night, and have breakfast the next morning. Your bill? 65 cents.

In 1850, Naperville was growing rapidly. According to the DuPage Census of the time, the area population was 1,226 - including "one Indian, and one Negro."

On Main Street, west side, just south of Jefferson Street, was the home of Judge Murray. He was a prominent, and powerful attorney in Naperville at that time. His was the home where Stephen Douglas spent the night when he and Abe Lincoln were in Naperville during the Lincoln / Douglas debates of 1856. Abe Lincoln did go on to win the republican nomination for the Illinois Senate.

While Stephen Douglas slept at Judge Murray's house, Abe Lincoln slept in the Pre-emption House Hotel. One story is that Lincoln gave an impromptu speech off the Pre-emption House roof. There is no official record of the speech, but there is written correspondence that refer to it happening.

Because slavery was a key issue in the debates, Lincoln's oft quoted sound bite from the debates probably rang out on Main street from the mouth of Abe Lincoln himself, "A house divided against itself cannot stand. I believe this government cannot endure permanently, half slave, half free."

Of course, back then the area was a lot different than now. The river was much larger than today, and most of the ground was marshy. In fact it was so muddy that if you got stuck in it, it could take hours to get yourself out. Animal life, too, was much more abundant, as were rattlesnakes – in the grass and in the river. The abundant wildlife continued for a long time; in the 1870's, a man speared an 11-pound eel in Mill Street pond (Mill Street pond is the portion of the Riverwalk that is directly behind the current Park District buildings on Jackson Street at Mill.) And in 1950, a man caught a 28-inch Northern Pike while fishing from the Main Street bridge.

By the late 1800s Naperville was really flourishing. There were two more major hotels - the Naper House Hotel and the Washington House. The Naperville School had 279 students and 147 books in its inventory. The average income in America at that time was 29 cents an hour.

In 1900 Naperville's population was 2,600 and illness was rampant. Thankfully, Bed Bugs, also in abundance, were considered a cure for many illnesses including fever, chills, hysteria, and sore eyes. They were often crushed to powder and mixed with human milk. At that time the 3rd leading cause of death in the U.S. was Diarrhea. Consumption (later called Tuberculosis, or TB) was also very common. An actual Consumption remedy was to swallow live baby frogs and drink a broth of boiled black cat! (It was believed that the secretions on the frogs had medicinal benefits). Medicines were virtually non-existent or primitive.

Hygiene, too, was an issue. In 1900, etiquette dictated that hair should be washed no less than once a month. Proper dress for young and middle-aged women was a skirt and white blouse or a dark muslin dress. These dresses were very heavy and uncomfortable, often containing over 10 yards of cloth. Men wore dark suits with stiff starched collars.

As the years passed and the century flipped, the first "autocar" in Naperville was seen on Washington Street, near Jefferson, in May 1905, probably driving from Chicago to Aurora.

In 1944, girls in Naperville outnumbered boys 2 to 1. And, in 1988, a study revealed that Naperville had over 96 different species of tree, more species than any other comparable Midwestern neighborhood.

If you look closely at downtown Naperville you'll notice two things that separate it from other business districts in the area:

1) Naperville is the only city in the area in which the railroad doesn't run through the middle of the downtown shopping area. This is because the powerful people who ran Naperville in the early days also owned the local toll road! It was called Plank Road. They resisted the railroad fiercely.

2) There are no telephone poles in downtown. This is because in 1910 when the roads began to be paved, forward-thinking city planners put the telephone cables *underground* - most cities didn't get around to this idea until 1980!

Naperville - Chicago's Haunted Neighbor

An Exploration into Naperville's Bizarre History and True Stories of its Unrested Dead

3rd Edition

HauntedNaperville.com

HauntedNaperville.com

Naperville Ghosts

Naperville's First Ghostly Encounter?

Naperville was only 35 years old when its first reported "ghostly encounter" caused a stir. It took place in Naperville's Vermont Cemetery.

Vermont Cemetery - on Normantown Road at 91st street - had already been in use for over 50 years when Joe Naper settled our town. The small burial ground is only 200 feet square. It boasts rare Illinois prairie plants, graves from the late 1700s, and at least one... *ghost.*

Today Vermont Cemetery is closed to visitors. The high chain link and barbed wire fence sends a powerful message to stay out. Within the fenced area, protected from public traffic, are some of America's oldest tombstones. Unfortunately, as efficient as the fence is at keeping intruders out, it appears to offer little resistance to an antsy anomaly eager to exit the cemetery for a stroll on Normantown Road...

The year was 1887. An elderly couple that lived near the cemetery was traveling in their horse and buggy along a dusty rocky path that is today Normantown Road. They'd spent the day visiting relatives in the near by western town of Oswego. They left their hosts at dusk, knowing they had enough time to get home before dark. Travel in the dark was extremely dangerous, as they were well aware. There could be many life-threatening forces between the two houses: marauding Indians, thieves, wild animals, insects, the pitch dark, and of course – ghosts.

They traveled eastbound on the dusty path as the sun was setting behind them. Then, on the road in the distance ahead of them, they spotted what appeared to be a man standing on the road near the entrance to the cemetery. Knowing it could be a dangerous situation; they were concerned as their buggy drew closer to the dark and mysterious figure - it appeared to be *waiting for them...*

As they drew upon him, what was left of the setting sun illuminated his face. They made eye contact with the man for an instant before the man turned away and began walking up the short path toward the cemetery gate. For a fleeting moment, the two riders felt relief for they recognized the man as a neighbor of theirs. Then their calm turned to terror as they realized that he was a neighbor whose funeral they had attended in Vermont Cemetery several months earlier!

In stunned shock, they watched him enter the cemetery gate and disappear before their eyes.

Now, if you're like me, you may be thinking that this story sounds more like folklore than an actual ghostly encounter. And I would agree with you, except for this...

More recently, a deputy sheriff who runs the overnight beat down the same road the elderly couple traveled on, claims that he has seen a human figure in the darkness on the road in front of the cemetery - at the same place the elderly couple had seen it! But, by the time the squad car reaches the spot, there is no one visible. Gone.

According to the police officer, it has happened several times. So, we have a visible anomaly whose description is similar to the 1887 anomaly, and it's seen at the same location - yet, the sightings *are over 120 years apart.*

Doesn't sound like folklore to me...

Naperville Ghosts

The Haunted Theater

The building at 34 W. Jefferson is the former Naperville Theater and Vaudeville stage. It was called the Grand Theater. This darkened antiquated building stands on land that during the late 1800s and early 1900s was occupied by two smaller buildings. Over the years those buildings housed a barbershop/bathhouse, bike shop, tailor, jewelry shop, insurance company, Chinese laundry, and a candy store, among others.

Then, in 1915, the two buildings were purchased and razed, and from the rubble rose the current structure, erected in 1916 at a cost of $37,158.80 - including $5,000.00 for 41 X 120 feet of prime Naperville real estate! The ground level had two storefronts separated by a 10-foot wide hallway that led to the Grand Movie Theater. The theater showed silent films to piano and organ accompaniment.

Silent movies on the schedule for January of 1920: "Sis Hopkins," "A Girl at Bay," "Go West Young Man," Mary Pickford in "Pollyanna," Charley (that's the way the advertisement spelled it) Chaplin in "A Day of Pleasure," and Harold Lloyd in "Haunted Spooks." Movies changed a couple times a week, in rotation.

The original Grand Theater building

Attendance numbers were low as early Napervillians considered motion pictures a questionable activity (much like the "devil's playground" activities of playing cards and dancing). In fact, many young people were forbidden from attending movie picture shows.

By 1930, between the Great Depression and Naperville's Blue Law (which prohibited unnecessary work and public performances on Sundays,) the Grand Theater was in financial dire straits and was forced to close. After the closing, a couple of furniture businesses failed here also. Then on August 14, 1935, just five years after the Grand Theater closed, a new sound movie theater opened, seating 460; it was named the Naper Theater. The first show was the film "Doubting Thomas."

Admission was 25 cents for adults and 10 cents for the tikes in tow; candy was a nickel. One of the first movies to show in the new Naper Theater was a classic of the undead, the original "Dracula" starring Bela Lugosi. Six years later, in 1939, "The Wizard of Oz" graced the screen, complete with live appearances in Naperville of the film's stars! For Halloween 1944, the Naper Theater showed a creepy double feature: "Henry Aldrich Haunts a House" and "Ghost Ship."

After a renovation in the 1950s, the theater sported seating up to 600, air conditioning, a larger concession area, and more gleaming aluminum. The newly installed marquee, located above the entrance, blinked with many flashing lights gleefully illuminating bustling Jefferson Avenue with the excitement Hollywood offered.

Double features were very popular in Naperville. Most often, they were terrible B movies and exploitation flicks. (Actually shown: "Pistol-Packin Mama" and "Girls in Chains"). The Intermission Restaurant was located across the street, where Potters restaurant currently is, so you could grab a bite to eat between double feature movies.

In June 1960, Alfred Hitchcock's "Psycho" terrified Napervillians like no film before it ever had. They would also show weekend movies featuring Shirley Temple, Jane Withers, Gene Autry, Hop-a-long Cassidy, and Roy Rogers. They ran weekly serial adventures, such as "Flash Gordon," "Buck Rogers," and "Son of the Guardsman."

Alas, as all good things must at sometime cease, the hallowed theater closed its doors in 1977 to be replaced by other stores and eventually an antique mall that quickly became a Naperville not-to- miss location. Sadly, it died in May of 2008. So many wonderful memories these walls hold, could there actually be ghosts in there?

HauntedNaperville.com

A Hollywood Honey

Might I call your attention to the front door of the theater as seen in the photo below?

The front door of the Haunted Theater

During an investigation inside this building, in April of 2008, it was discovered, about 20 feet inside the front door, a delightful spirit we've come to call Marilyn the Hollywood Honey.

Now, if you were standing at the doorway this moment, you might peer eagerly inside hoping for a glimpse of this restless rascal from another realm, and I would in no way discourage your quest because I know that a minimum of two dimensions converge on that unassuming space. Yes, there exists on that spot a ghostly starlet of sorts. A ditsy headed Hollywood honey who spends her eternity preparing for her next show - never realizing that the "production of her life" was a play that closed all too quickly -- perhaps so quickly she's not aware it ended at all...

Marilyn is perhaps drawn to the spot because of the energy of the former theater. She appeared to a psychic. The starlet was rummaging through dresses as if she were in a dressing room backstage of a playhouse. She saw the psychic and acknowledged her, by nodding toward her. The psychic asked her what she was doing. She responded, "It's Showtime!"

The psychic asked the starlet her name. She mumbled something that wasn't very clear; it sounded like Nanette or Margaret. The psychic asked again. At that point, the starlet appeared somewhat frustrated. She shook her head, snapping, "Just call me Marilyn."

With that she faded away.

Spot in Antique Store where Hollywood Honey appeared

HauntedNaperville.com

In assembling her story, I would conclude that Marilyn is most certainly a tragic ghost - perhaps the saddest type of all. Because of her young age, about 25, and the fact that she haunts a small theater in Naperville, she in all likelihood met with a tragic end. In piecing this together, it would appear that Marilyn was probably a Naperville girl with a dream, probably to be like her idol - the Hollywood superstar, Marilyn Monroe.

I would surmise that, while living, she'd spent many happy hours in this theater, dreaming of the day when she'd be a star and on the screen for others to enjoy. She may have headed to Hollywood in the late 1950s, because this is when Marilyn Monroe was most popular and appeared in movies shown on the Naperville screen.

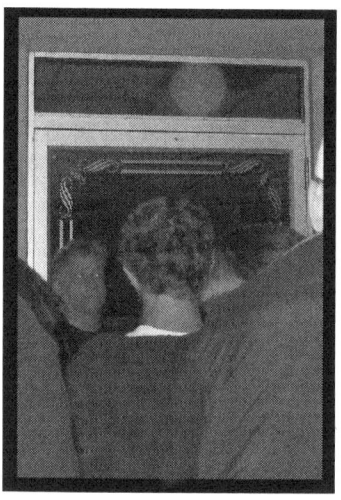

Note the large orb <u>inside the locked theater</u>!
It appeared while Kevin told the Hollywood Honey story
to a group on his tour.   Photo by Kristi Roepke

I wish I could speculate that all Hollywood stole was her dream. But, because of the nature of this haunt, my conviction is otherwise. I believe Marilyn met with a terrible and violent end while chasing her dream - a vicious murder or perhaps death at her own hands. (According to many, Marilyn Monroe probably met her end in one of these two ways as well).

Our Hollywood Honey, believing that the show must go on, continues to go on, taking up residence here where she feels most at home.

Here in the place where her dreams of stardom were planted and energized - in her hometown theater on Naperville's Jefferson Street.

Playing it Safe

The building at 34 West Jefferson that housed the movie theaters has several ghostly encounters to boast about. And that's not surprising considering its past - it's almost as if the building was destined to become "creepy-city."

When the Grand Theater in this building closed in 1930, Kriebs-Wilmes leased the location for their new department store. They planned to sell appliances on the ground level and store the inventory in the basement. Of course, this was going to be a problem; appliances in those days were very solid, sturdy and heavy, very difficult to bring downstairs for storage and then back up to ground level when sold. The answer was an elevator. So an elevator was installed to move the inventory more easily between floors.

Unfortunately, money was tight and the only elevator that was within the budget of the new business was a coffin elevator! These were the type used in funeral establishments and morgues. They lacked the style of consumer elevators, no finished walls for instance. The unit was more like a freight elevator of today - very raw, no frills, no walls or ceiling, just steel framework. The floor, too, is steel.

Haunted theater's rare Coffin Elevator

What separates the coffin elevator from a freight elevator most visually is its shape - it is quite unique and strange. The coffin elevator is designed to carry oblong cargo, such as a coffin, so it is about eight feet wide and only three feet deep!

It was peculiar, for sure. But it was affordable and it worked. Unfortunately it may have set the stage for this building to foster the macabre...

On Jefferson street, there is a door at 34 West Jefferson that, when opened, exposes a set of stairs that lead down. This is a sublevel retail store that is actually located in the basement of the former theater.

The retail space is unique - exposed rafters, concrete walls, narrow passageways, low ceiling, and limited light. There is a wonderful candle shop here in this area of the building, and in one dark corner of the shop is a strange object with a secret of its own - it's a safe with a ghost.

This is the safe that was originally in Naperville's first bank/city hall/jail at 18 West Jefferson (currently the Francesca's Restaurant). This safe was the bank's safe.

The safe is a large walk-in type, constructed entirely of heavy steel. It was not part of the original construction of the 34 West Jefferson building in 1916. It is believed that the safe was moved to this building either by the furniture business in 1930 or the theater in 1935. Didn't the movers notice the freeloading ghost?

Mike and Donna used to own a soy candle business in this sublevel retail space. It was an adorable shop and a Naperville gem. They love the building, and they had never considered the safe suspicious. But one day in 2006 all that changed.

In 2006, Donna was assisting a customer. Donna had her back to the safe as she was speaking to the customer. Several times during their discussion, the customer would grimace and appear to be looking over Donna's shoulder.

After a few times, Donna asked the woman, "Is there something wrong?" The woman leaned in and whispered, "Who is that man in the safe who keeps watching us?"
Donna was confused. "What man?" She turned around toward the safe. The safe door was only ajar about 10 inches. She saw no one. The customer said, "There's a man in the safe. He's about 5'9" with dark hair. He keeps peeking out at us."
Donna shook her head in befuddlement, motioned for the woman to follow her, and began walking toward the safe.

As they reached the safe, they cautiously peered inside without opening the door any further. From that vantage point, they couldn't see anyone. It was eerily quiet. Donna quickly swung the safe door open and the women jumped back - in case the man was to run out. Nothing. They stepped forward and wholly examined the interior of the safe. It was empty.

The 100-year-old concrete was silent.

The customer defended herself. "He was here. I saw him several times! Is there another way out? Could he leave?"
Donna shook her head '*no*.'
The customer said, "Then you've got a ghost."

That is the only known appearance of the safe ghost. That is until one day, about 18 months later, when a psychic walked into the antique store upstairs. As soon as she walked in, she felt him in the building. She immediately made her way through the maze of stairs and corridors all the way to the safe in the basement. Note: She walked directly to the safe, and this was her first time in the building. She hadn't even been told about the safe or the ghost story!

She approached the safe and said, "You don't have to be afraid. It's okay." She turned to the others present and said, "He just ran to the other room." She followed him. From the other room, the psychic was heard talking to him. She was asking him what he was afraid of.

After a moment, she emerged from the room. She said that the spirit's name is Nathan and he's very scared, but he wouldn't tell her what he was scared of. Whenever she asked him what he was afraid of, he would answer "Get Jean (Gene)." When the psychic asked him who Jean (Gene) was, all Nathan would say is "Get Jean (Gene)." We do not know if Nathan was speaking of a female Jean or a male Gene.

Later, while discussing Nathan with the psychic, I asked her to describe him. She leaned back and smiled. "He's about 40 years old. He's wearing a dark blue or black pea coat. He may be in the armed services. He's about 5'10". His hair is very, very, dark."

The psychic's description matched the original customer's description of the man *exactly*.

The safe where the ghost of Nathan appears.

HauntedNaperville.com

The Streets of Naperville

Ace Keller

The date was Thursday, August 10th, 1922. This is the date that two Naperville sons, LeRoy Keller and Edwin Schillo, were killed in a plane crash that occurred smack dab in the heart of what is today downtown Naperville.

LeRoy Keller was part of a Naperville pioneer family, and was flying to the outskirts of Naperville to his parent's farm to have dinner with his family. Accompanying him in the aircraft was his great friend and fellow pilot Edwin Schillo, who was at the time the President of Schillo Motor sales on Michigan Avenue in Chicago.

Napervillians enjoyed watching the spectacular aircraft maneuvers of Keller, who would often entertain the gathering crowds below him when he would fly over Naperville. We was considered an ace in the cockpit and always put on an amazing show.

Arriving over Naperville at about 7pm, Keller began a series of thrilling aircraft stunts. As usual he was wowing the crowd below.

The awe and wow of the crowd only lasted a moment before the scene suddenly began to play out in slow motion horror as the spectators realized that something was very wrong - *the plane had begun a rapid decent directly toward the rows of homes below.*

The crowd could see that Keller was putting the safety of the town ahead of his own, as they could see him making every effort possible to guide his crippled craft in such a way as to avoid hitting the residential area. With unparalleled skill, Keller managed to guide his plummeting craft away from the homes and toward the quarry (currently the Paddleboat Lake.) The plane violently crashed on West Street, just east of the quarry and north of Aurora Avenue - missing the residential area, and crashing just a few feet from the quarry.

The Naperville Quarry, before it became Paddleboat Lake.

With the crash came the horrific explosion of the gas tank as sheets of flame enveloped the craft and unfortunate flyers. The heat from the explosion was so intense that rescuing the men was impossible. The fire department was called, but the plane and passengers were reduced to smoldering ashes in a matter of a moment.

LeRoy Keller was born in Naperville to George and Ida Keller, at their farm south and west of Naperville, on July 25, 1894. He enlisted in the army in 1917 and was attached to the 325 Aero Squadron. He was honorable discharged in 1919. On June 22, 1920 he was married to Ruth Burchal.

Keller is the grandson of Naperville pioneer families Keller and Yackley. He left behind a widow and a son of eight months.

HauntedNaperville.com

The Streets of Naperville

The Prestidigitation of The Mysterious Smith

We all know colleges are haunted. We all know theaters are haunted. So what hope does a college theater have?

The North Central College Theater is named Pfeiffer Hall and it stands on the southeast corner of Benton and Brainard Streets. It was built in 1926 at a cost of $230,000.

Most Napervillians are aware of the fine live shows produced on this stage each season, but few know that when it was built it also functioned as a movie theater as well. The first film shown was "Robin Hood" starring Douglas Fairbanks, on Friday, May 31, 1926.

Oh, and like any theater worth its salt - it's *haunted.*

Haunted by as many as ten ghosts, depending whom you choose to believe...

But this isn't a story of ghostly visitation. This is a story of magic, trickery, illusion, and mind reading. This is the tale of Naperville's encounter with magician extraordinaire – The Mysterious Smith.

When chronicling the magicians of the early 20th century, Harry Houdini and Blackstone come to mind readily - but there are others, among them, The Mysterious Smith.

It was September 9, 1929, a few years after the death of Harry Houdini, that The Mysterious Smith graced the stage of Pfeiffer Hall and dazzled early Napervillians with fetes of deft manipulation.

It was a Thursday night. The build-up and hype had been extraordinary. This was not a show to miss! It was a unique Vaudeville performance that performed to rave reviews all over the U.S. Now it was Naperville's turn.

The show was performed in Naperville in three parts. In the first part, Mysterious Smith performed illusions that left the occupants of Pfeiffer Hall breathless. They included the "Catching a Fish in Mid-Air" illusion, and the "Rat in a Wine Bottle," among others.

The second part of the show was a mind reading extravaganza by Madame Olga. A week before the show, readers of the Naperville Clarion newspaper were encouraged to send a mystifying question to the paper for Madame Olga to divine an answer for. She would answer a handful in print in the paper before the show came to town. The others would have to attend the show to get their answers! And attend they did!

Between 1929 and 1931, Madame Olga's performance was all the rage, often playing to standing-room-only crowds.

For the third and final portion of the show, Mysterious Smith would return to the stage pulling an actual casket behind him! He would then be fitted into a straight jacket and locked in the casket. A curtain was drawn up, and less than two minutes later, Mysterious Smith emerged from behind the curtain! He'd throw the straight jacket across the stage while the open casket sat empty center stage. It was as if he'd cheated death! The audience roared with applause.

Most people weren't aware that Mysterious Smith and Olga were married, but in this area, we knew them as Mr. & Mrs. A.P. Smith of Warrenville, where they resided during their time off.

Alas, unfortunately, the Great Depression took its toll on attendance numbers for The Mysterious Smith Show, and the duo vanished from the road by 1934.

Mysterious Smith had a respectable decade as a highly respected performer in "magician circles." He even produced a program in 1926 partnering with Harry Houdini entitled: "3 Shows in One - Magic, Escapes, and Fraud Mediums Exposed."

Mysterious Smith Show Program and Autographed Photo

HauntedNaperville.com

Naperville Ghosts

I Want to Be a Fireman

Sitting on the river's edge, the building at 48 West Chicago Avenue is much more than it seems from the outside. The front of the building sits on Chicago Avenue. Originally this was called Water Street, and it was the main street in town. As the town grew north, Jefferson Street became the center of town and Naperville's primary business street, as it is today.

Front of building on Chicago Avenue

The back of the building sits dangerously close to the unpredictable river. In the early days of Naperville this branch of the DuPage river was much larger, and it wasn't unusual for the summer to bring flooding, and the winter to bring briskly floating sheets of ice that obliterated anything in their path, including trees, homes and businesses. The river was confined to its current size by solid walls constructed in 1889.

Upon entering the building there's a dark, almost claustrophobic, feeling – like traveling in the suffocating quarters of a ship's hull. Of course, that feeling is only reinforced as you move toward the back of the building, and the ominous waters of the river seem strangely close outside the windows, as if you're glaring out the portholes of a vessel at sea.

I suppose it's not unusual then that the most popular ghost story tied to the building deals with water and the river...

Back in the 1980s, this location was a very popular restaurant. One of the many employees of the business was a young man named Robert, working as a waiter. As the story is told, the restaurant had closed for the night, and Robert and a few others were preparing to close up the place. There was much to do in the kitchen as well as the dining areas. Robert's job was to clean and vacuum the dining area along the windows that overlook the river.

Robert was alone in the room – or so he thought. He was busy carrying out his duties when suddenly, from the corner of his eye, he thought he saw a tablecloth moving on a table off to his right. He turned and looked – nothing there. The tablecloth was still. He shrugged it off and went back to work. A moment later, again from the corner of his eye, he saw the movement a second time. He turned off the vacuum and the room was eerily quiet. He stared at the table for a moment. There! It moved again, only this time he definitely *saw it move!*

He walked up to it, pulled the tablecloth to the side, and peered beneath. To his amazement, a small boy sat under there! He was about four years old and had a toy fire hose in his hands.

Robert asked, "Who are you?"
The boy said, "I want to be a fireman!" And with that, he squeezed the toy fire hose, causing water to trickle out of the hose onto the floor.
Robert smiled, "Where are your parents?"
The boy responded, "They're not here."
Robert asked, "They left you here?"
The boy shot back angrily, "They're not here!"

Robert assumed that the boy's parents didn't leave the restaurant without him. The only reasonable explanation is that one of his parents worked for the restaurant and was still in the building. Robert told the boy to wait under the table, and he went to find the parent.

Robert questioned everyone working, but no other employee in the building knew of the boy. Robert and a couple of other employees went back to the table to get the lost boy. Robert pulled the tablecloth aside and there was no one there. The co-workers looked at Robert. He defended himself, "The kid was right there! I swear! He must be here somewhere."

Everyone began looking for the boy, but he was nowhere to be found - all doors were locked from the inside. After a few jokes about "Robert working too hard lately," the co-workers went back to their duties.

Robert, alone again, sat down next to the table thinking he was going crazy. He peered under the table one more time. The boy still wasn't there, but that's when he saw it - a small piece of carpet appeared damp. He touched it. It *was wet*. It was wet from the fire hose water! The boy *had* been there.

Other employees encountered the boy on several other occasions after that. There are also reports, up to this day, that cold drafts can be felt in the dining area where the boy had been seen.

The Boy Ghost has appeared just inside these windows, in the dining area.

So who is he?

We can't be sure at this point, but there is an interesting "coincidence" in Naperville's history that could shed light on this haunt. The date was Sunday, December 2, 1953. Two children - Jean Peterson, age 6, and Edward Rosenstiel, age 3 - were playing in Eddie's backyard, which happened to be on the riverfront at 203 Water Street.

The two children went missing. In the following days and weeks, one of the nation's largest searches was instituted right here in Naperville. The river was scoured top to bottom for miles in either direction with no success. It was surmised that perhaps the children had fallen into the river and were dragged, by the river flow, into the quarry that is today the Paddleboat Lake. (This story echoed hauntingly familiar in Naperville: 38 years earlier, in July of 1915, a 12 year old child named Carl Kibbler had drowned mysteriously in the same quarry; then, in June of 1926, the quarry claimed another life, that of Glenn Girard.)

Crews and equipment were quickly brought in. The lake was completely drained, all 80 million gallons of it! Still there was no trace of the children.

As a bitter winter set in, the search efforts were called off. Then, at 10:04 a.m., February 3, 1954, a utility worker named Richard Forrestal was working on a transformer along the river at Webster Street when he noticed, under the surface ice of the water, what appeared to be a doll's face. As he looked closer, it was clear to him that it wasn't a doll at all - it was the *face of a child*.

He quickly notified the authorities.

Upon inspection, it was determined to be the missing Jean Peterson child. Her playmate, little Edward Rosenstiel, was discovered under the ice just 56 feet away. Both children still wore the same clothing they were wearing when reported missing. Although the children had tragically perished, all of Naperville thanked God for their discovery and the closure it brought.

Subsequent tests concluded:
1) The children had not been molested.
2) The food in their stomachs was the same as they'd eaten right before their disappearances.
3) They were still wearing the same clothing as when they went missing.
4) Their bodies showed decomposition consistent with being in the water for months.

So, of course, a massive mystery emerged: How did the children return to the place where they first went missing? The spot had been searched countless times by thousands of volunteers and professionals. And with the water being just 4.5 inches deep, there is no way they could have overlooked the bodies. So where had the children been during the months of searching? *And, how did they get back to what was basically the exact spot where they had vanished 59 days earlier?*

All these questions remain a mystery to this day.

And another mystery - is the young ghost with the fire hose that of Edward Rosenstiel? It seems an incredible coincidence that a small boy, the same age as Edward, haunts a building near the spot where Edward died. Is it possible that young Edward has found some sort of comfort in this building? Had he been in the building with his parents when he was alive?

We will try to update this investigation in future editions of this book.

HauntedNaperville.com

The Streets of Naperville

Movie and a Murder

The throws of the depression brought the echo of murderous gunshot to the quiet town of Naperville, in a story of lost love and jealousy. And when the gun cooled, Naperville found itself with the cold-blooded murder of a beautiful young lady by a jilted boyfriend driven to vacant desperation.

March 21, 1929, was the day a series of unfortunate events, four years in the making, culminated in the death of 23-year-old Margaret Weismantel, the daughter of Naperville's first mail carrier, Joseph Weismantel, and his wife Eva.

It began in the summer of 1925...

The train pulled into the Naperville station right on time. Theodore was on his own and it felt good. He was anxious to start a new life. He'd made mistakes recently, most notably a few burglaries. They cost him two years of his freedom. His hometown of Cape Gerardo, Missouri had grown old, and his overbearing train engineer father – stifling. Twenty-year-old Theodore needed a fresh start and a change, a place where he could put his past behind him. He'd heard good things about Naperville: it was clean, there was work, they welcomed outsiders, and, of course, the important things – girls outnumbered boys, and the teenagers enjoyed skinny dipping in the river. Theodore packed his bag and boarded the train.

As the train came to a stop, Theodore watched Naperville unfold through the window. He felt a rush. He could see the Kroehler furniture manufacturing building off to the east. They employed over 900 people in that place - paid well too. Though the thought of lugging furniture from the factory to the train didn't thrill him, it was a starting place. He'll visit the manager tomorrow.

He stepped out onto the platform and squinted at the bright sun as he looked west. His first order of business - lodging. He lit a cigarette and proceeded to Washington Street.

Theodore was young and strong, two qualities the management of Kroehler manufacturing never turned away. Theodore found himself employed quickly. Loading trucks, though, didn't cut it for him, so he worked hard always keeping an eye open for a driving job. Driving a delivery truck was much more appealing to him. It took a year. Theodore was moving up.

During this year, Theodore attracted the attention of several young ladies in Naperville, but there was one he especially liked. She worked at the Kroehler plant, too. At first he knew her only as "the clerk girl with the curly hair." Then one day they started an awkward conversation, she introduced herself as Margaret Weismantel. He told her his name was Theodore, Theodore Freeman. They hit it off.

She liked the idea that he was a doer. He wasn't happy in Missouri, so he moved; he wasn't happy loading trucks, so he worked harder and was promoted. This guy is different. He takes action. Margaret liked that about him. She could love him.

Margaret's father, Joseph, had also worked at the plant. He was one of their first employees, back in 1899. Now he was a mail carrier in Naperville. In fact, he was Naperville's first mail carrier, having started his route in 1906. Margaret introduced Theodore to her father and informed him that Theodore would like to take her out. Joe consented.

For the next two years, things went well for Theodore and Margaret - even Margaret's mother and sisters liked Theodore. Their love grew and they made plans for the future. They made friends, namely Allen Hock, a young barber in town, Richard Albrecht, and Mr. & Mrs. Horbelt. Things were good. Of course there was that one thing, the thing about Theodore that rubbed everyone the wrong way. No one spoke about it, but everyone was concerned about it - Theodore had a temper, a bad temper. In most cases the impetus for the outbursts was jealousy - jealousy for anyone associating with Margaret.

For two years most people accepted Theodore, temper and all. They understood his frustration. After all, Margaret was a beautiful girl, and there was always the chance that her next casual conversation with a boy could leave Theodore in the cold. Everyone, including Theodore, knew it could happen at any time. His fear grew and manifested itself in more frequent and more abusive bursts.

About 2-1/2 years into their courtship, Joseph happened to walk in the house to find Theodore screaming and ranting at Margaret in a completely rude, uncontrolled, disrespectful, and unacceptable fashion. Margaret appeared genuinely frightened. Joe put his foot down - Theodore was no longer allowed in the house. Completely unwelcome, Theodore stormed out.

At that point, Joe had a talk with his daughter Margaret. He advised her to stop this association, to break it off. She said that he was right, but the problem was that she still loved Theodore. She couldn't bear to let him go.

She went to her room.

Joe, a devout Catholic, sat in the now-quiet living room and prayed for his family.

As the months went by, Margaret found Theodore's behavior more and more erratic. She grew to dislike being with him. His behavior was also a problem at work, and in December of 1928 he found himself without a job.

When he told Margaret of his situation, she knew that there was no way they could start their family anytime soon. Both of their lives had been put on hold. And unfortunately for Theodore, he was no longer worth waiting for. Margaret broke it off.

Theodore had lost the two things most important to him in the world: his work and Margaret. He fell into despair. He tried finding other work, but, in such a small town, his despondency and angry reputation preceded him. Weeks went by; he lost his apartment. Thankfully a friend of his, Richard Albrecht, who worked as a firefighter and with the police, had an apartment above the firehouse. The building adjoined the police headquarters building. Both buildings were on the southeast corner where Jefferson Street crosses Webster Street. Theodore began sleeping there and had full access to both buildings.

Margaret would occasionally meet with Theodore and give him cigarette money. He'd lost everything, and she couldn't bear to see him try to get through it without his smokes, too.

On March 20, 1929, Margaret met up with Theodore. She asked how things were going, but she could tell that he wasn't doing well at all. All he wanted was to win her back. All she wanted was to get away from him. She mentioned that she was going to the movies later that night with her friends, Mr. & Mrs. Horbelt. She was looking forward to it.

Theodore remembered the happier times when he and Margaret would go to the movies. She'd hold his hand. He wanted that back so badly. He asked if it was just the three of them going. She answered yes. He was hoping she'd invite him. She didn't. She gave him 45 cents for cigarettes and left.

Margaret went home to get ready. While there, the Horbelt's called - the Weismantel phone number was 111 - to ask if Dean Perry, a friend of Margaret's from High School, could join the festivities tonight. Margaret had been out with Dean on a couple other occasions, but she made it clear that this wouldn't be a date. They all agreed.

A short time later, a car's horn beeped outside, Margaret peered through the curtains. It was the Horbelt's Hudson Coach, and it looked like Dean was in the back seat. She kissed her parents good night, waved 'bye' to her younger sisters, Marie, Francis, and Agnes, and headed out.

The ride to the theater from the Weismantel home on Mill Street was only a couple minutes. They went right into the theater. They saw a comedy called "The Flying Feet," starring Romen Novarro, Ralph Graves, and Anita Page.

Theodore, at this time, was festering. He couldn't shake the feeling that Margaret had lied to him. She was on a date; he could feel it. He called his friend Allen Hock to suggest a night of drunkenness. Hock liked the idea. He picked up Theodore and they drove to Aurora to purchase a pint of liquor and six bottles of lemon pop. They opened the pop and spiked it with the alcohol.

Soon the topic turned to Margaret. Theodore convinced his friend to drive past her house. Then they circled around and drove by again. The light in her bedroom was still out; she's not home yet. They went to Wilson's Restaurant in downtown Naperville. Hock drove himself home from there, leaving Theodore to walk the short distance west on Jefferson Street to his apartment in the police/fire buildings.

As Theodore was walking west down Jefferson Street, he paused across the street from the movie theater as the movie was letting out. He couldn't believe what he saw – Margaret, the Horbelt's, and Perry! They were laughing and smiling and having just a grand old time. They were probably laughing about Theodore! Poor Theodore has nothing! What a loser! His mind was spinning. How could she do this to me? She lied to me. She'll regret it. She'll regret it...

He ran back to the police station. His friend Albrecht was seated at the desk. They exchanged a few pleasant words. Then Theodore pretended to go upstairs but instead slipped into the coatroom. He began to quickly rummage through the police uniforms and coats. It didn't take long to find what he was looking for – a pistol, police issue. It was Albrecht's. Theodore slid it in his belt and slinked out onto Jefferson Street.

It was dark and quiet.

He looked both ways to see if anyone had seen him. Nope. Margaret lived two blocks west, on Mill Street, between Jefferson and Benton. He quickly began to run to her house, all the while rehearsing how he'd scare all of them with the gun. They'll learn a lesson about messing with Theodore Freeman.

When he got to the house he could see that they weren't back yet. He hid in the bushes under the front window of the house. He wasn't there long. To the south, on Jefferson, he saw a car turn right, its headlights glaring, coming north on Mill. The car came to a stop in front of Margaret's house. They put the car in park and seemed to be talking about something. He could see Margaret in the back seat – with Perry.

Theodore burst out of the bushes, screaming at Margaret. Everyone in the car was mildly shocked at first, and then they noticed, reflected in the moonlight, the pistol in Theodore's hand. Shock turned to terror as each realized that they were ducks in a barrel if Freeman decided to release his rage through the trigger under his finger. They all trembled as he raged on - his eyes gazing off to a place only he could see.

Then he pointed the gun into the back seat.

Before anyone could reason that he'd *never really shoot them* – four shots rang out - one right after the other. Mrs. Horbelt screamed. Mr. Horbelt fumbled for the keys in the ignition. Dean grabbed his shoulder in pain and Margaret fell onto Dean's lap unconscious.

Theodore let out a scream as if a demon were escaping.

Yelling for Margaret, Theodore tore open the passenger door and jumped in the back seat. He held Margaret the way he used to. Rocking her, he cried, "Please don't die. I'm sorry. Please. Please."

He told Mr. Horbelt to get them to Dr. Simpson's office, at 40 East Jefferson, quickly. The nearest hospital was St. Charles Hospital in Aurora, much too far to get care for the victims. As they were pulling out, Mr. Weismantel, who'd heard the shots, came running out. Mrs. Horbelt yelled, "Margaret's been shot, we're going to Simpson's office."

Joe Weismantel jumped into his car and began following the Horbelts. As the Horbelt's turned right onto Benton they accelerated briskly, catching the attention of Naperville Police Officer Ruckert. He, not realizing the danger of the situation, began to follow what he perceived as simply two speeding vehicles. He followed them all the way to Simpson's office on east Jefferson Street.

Upon arrival, he became aware of the assault. He arrested Freeman. Doctor Simpson called for the Beidelman ambulance to take the seriously injured Margaret to St. Charles Hospital; there was little he could do for her. Margaret had been shot twice in the chest. Perry had been shot in the shoulder, the bullet passing through. The other bullet was unaccounted for. Mr. Weismantel joined Perry and Margaret in the ambulance ride to Aurora.

Margaret died in her father's arms en route.

Officer Ruckert brought Freeman to the police station. Freeman's friend, Richard Albrecht, was seated at the reception desk. Unaware of the situation, he looked curiously at the two men. Freeman walked up to the desk, reached into his pocket, removing the 45 cents he'd received from Margaret earlier in the day. He put it on the desk, saying, "I won't be needing this money where I'm goin'."

The next day the sleepy town of Naperville reeled from the news.

Freeman immediately confessed his guilt to the state's attorney, asking that they not tell his mother what he'd done. While held without bond in the county jail in Wheaton, Freeman begged to see Margaret's body. The authorities refused.

At the four-day trial, Freeman, taking the stand, claimed he had no recollection of the shooting - only the incidents leading up to it and then holding Margaret in the back seat of the car.

The jury of 12 men agreed on Freeman's guilt with their first ballot. The difficulty came in determining his sentence. Three ballots were taken before a decision was reached. The jury was free to choose the death penalty but chose not to.

In a curious twist reflecting a Christian attitude seldom witnessed, Margaret's father refused to help prosecute Freeman. He said, "The boy has parents too, and another death won't bring our Margaret back." He went on to say that Freeman "has problems and he hopes the boy gets help."

Ultimately, Freeman was found guilty of second-degree murder in a Wheaton court and was sentenced to 35 years. His whereabouts today are unknown.

Margaret's funeral service was held in Saints Peter and Paul Church on Saturday, March 23, at 9:30 a.m., the Rev. F. Schildgen officiating. Margaret rests in the parish cemetery.

Naperville Ghosts

Naperville's Phantom

I have made a study of Naperville's ghosts for almost a decade. In that time I have participated in many dozens of professional paranormal investigations, as well as thousands of hours spent in research with my face buried in Naperville history. I have come to the conclusion that, by and large, Naperville's ghosts are not malicious. They appear to be lost, frightened, and generally no more dangerous than any other disembodied spirits.

But, I would be remiss - if not negligent - if I didn't warn you about Naperville's *one dark entity*. This is a very unrested soul. Not demonic, mind you - it was at one time a human. It roams Naperville's streets to this day, and, it is very angry -- more angry than is customary with "simple" ghosts. Over the years it has come to be called "Phantom" or "Shadow." I prefer Phantom because I think this thing is much more dastardly and diabolical than the name Shadow connotes.

In my opinion, this creature appears to have purpose, power, and personality, more like a Phantom. I'll refer to it as Phantom.

Many Napervillians over the years have had personal encounters with Phantom. Those who have been unfortunate enough to encounter phantom claim it is a thick black smoke-like entity that appears from out of nowhere. They say it is over seven feet tall, towering over them. They say that it exudes a heavy feeling of deep dark evil and foreboding. They say the air gets very cold in its presence. They say that when it's before you, you experience a depth of fear you have never experienced on earth before. They say that when it moves it appears to be wearing some sort of cloak and something that hides its face. But when standing still, it's more like thick black smoke that wraiths, undulates, or... *breathes.*

HauntedNaperville.com

It remains for about a minute and than vanishes as quickly as it had come. It has appeared outdoors as well as inside homes just like yours. It comes at all times of day – broad daylight appearances have been cataloged as well as occurrences of The Phantom appearing at the foot of a bed in the wee morning hours. Those who have experienced it claim that they have been "changed" by it, and that they will never forget it. We have no protection from it, and it can appear to anyone, anywhere, at any time.

It's like some sort of terrifying horror movie.
But, it's *not* a movie. *It's really here, in Naperville.*

So, who is the Phantom? Why is it here? Why does it torment this town?

Before we tackle this dilemma, let's look at some of the appearances of the Phantom over the years...

He's Been Seen Outside...

March 1929. A scalding summer was taking its toll on everyone in the Midwest. But the people in DuPage county had an additional burden to bear: a malevolent ghost. This was a ghost so cunning and elusive that the people were helpless and the police were useless.

The news quickly spread through the area. Some were calling it a ghost; some said it's a man seven feet tall; all were afraid to leave their houses.

It all started when a 14-year-old girl, who was playing in her back yard after dinner, came running into her house screaming to her parents that a "big black thing" was in the yard! They ran out see what the problem was and came face to face with what they described as a massive black shadow. It hovered around the yard giving off a cold breeze.

They were frozen in fear and shock. After a moment it took off through the other yards like a bullet.

Shortly after, a police report was filed by a youth club claiming that a "dark misty ugly face" was seen peering in their window.

The police reports said, whatever it is it knows its way around. Whenever it was pursued it moved "swift as a deer" and vanished into the night.

Another time two police officers thought they spotted the shadow in the back yard of a home, three shots were fired and the shadow disappeared like a streak. Then, according to police reports, undeterred at being shot at, he was back in that same yard the following night!

All summer no one dared leave his or her home alone.

When the weather cooled, the Shadow appearances stopped.

For now.

HauntedNaperville.com

He's Been Seen Inside...

September, 2006. The Naperville house is almost 125 years old. From its classic architecture, beautifully landscaped grounds, and authentic exterior color motif, one would never suspect for a moment something so dark could dwell within the walls...

The home's owner, Mrs. McCall (not her real name,) had just finished final touches to her family room. She had it meticulously gutted and rebuilt beautifully into a bar/theater room. She called several friends and asked them to come over and "break-in" the home's new entertainment area. The focal point of the redesign was a custom-made bar section - a spectacular Victorian-inspired masterpiece, with a large mirror running along the wall the entire length behind the bar. Ten vintage-inspired wooden stools surrounded the bar.

On the other side of the room was a home theater system and several new recliner chairs. The room was definitely an oasis from the madness of life - at least that was its intended purpose...

Mrs. McCall and five friends were enjoying the room. She and three of her friends were sitting at the bar talking, and two other friends had made themselves comfortable in the theater area's recliner chairs. The afternoon was progressing delightfully. Everyone was having a great time.

That is until the TV turned on all by itself - and not on a channel with programming, just simply loud white static distortion – an unheard-of situation in the digital age. The creepy and unexpected noise filled the room with a strange sense of uncertainty. Out of nervousness all the women started to laugh when their hostess exclaimed, "I guess we've got spooks here!" The nervous laughter continued for about ten seconds and then no one laughed....

They all noticed that the temperature in the room was plummeting! The women stared at each other in disbelief, but the nightmare wasn't over yet, not even close. Suddenly, a large black Shadow entity flew through the room - between the women at the bar and the women seated in the recliners. But, he wasn't visible to their eyes; he was only visible by his reflection in the large mirror behind the bar! He was large, dark, and had the appearance of a caped hooded figure moving very fast.

The women were speechless as he swiftly moved across the room.

As he passed through, the temperature in the room dropped even further. Then, as he vanished from sight, in an instant, the previous room temperature restored. And, according to Mrs. McCall, it wasn't even a gradual temperature return; as soon as he was gone, it was instantly about 70 degrees in the room again.

The women looked at each other in shock, and then they all ran out of the house into the backyard. Outside, and visibly shaken, they discussed what happened and they realized that they had all experienced the exact same thing! It actually happened, this was not in their imagination. They all saw the *same thing* - the Phantom.

To this day, Mrs. McCall doesn't use the newly finished area in her beautiful home; she only watches TV in her bedroom. And, she says, she and her friends have agreed to never again talk among themselves about what happened that afternoon. But, she injects, "I still get have an occasional nightmare about it."

HauntedNaperville.com

He's in Every Corner of Naperville...

In the course of doing my Naperville ghost tours, many tour participants share their ghostly encounters with me; they are of course varied and incredible tales. Some people speak of haunted furniture, strange recurring dreams, soldiers and Indians appearing in their home, strange yet familiar aromas, and more. But no tale is more common within Naperville's city limits than tales of personal encounters with Phantom. Here are a few examples:

A young man told me that, once, when he was having a sleepover at his house with some friends, back in about 1976, a "Phantom-like" entity moved through the room he and his friends were "camped out" in. He said that they all saw it. He said, "It scared the %#&@ out of us!" He never knew what it was until he heard about it on my tour.

A lady on my tour told me that she and her daughter, then seven years old, in 1982, were in their kitchen in the middle of the afternoon, rolling dough for cookies. She said that the room got freezing cold in an instant and "a thing like the Phantom" moved through the kitchen terrifying both of them. She said that after that day they never talked about it again, until last year. She said that her daughter, now in her 30s, was over for Christmas. After dinner, they were reminiscing about the old days and her daughter asked if "that ghost thing when we were making cookies" really happened or had she dreamed it? Her mother replied that it most certainly DID happen.

A married couple, that took my tour, shared an encounter with the Phantom that they had while staying in an old Naperville motel!

A woman who works at a Chiropractic office in Naperville told me that they have seen a "Phantom-like-thing" in their office many times over the years.

There are stories of a dark Phantom-like entity in the Naperville Cemetery.

A woman who lives in the Brookdale subdivision on Naperville's north side, told me that she and her husband have seen a Phantom-like entity in their home and back yard.

A man in the Cress Creek subdivision, on Naperville's north side, told me that he and his family have seen the Phantom in their home several times. The man thinks the Phantom has a "thing" for his 13-year-old daughter! This because every time they've seen it, it is "hanging around" her!

The Phantom has been seen several times in the 5th Avenue Station building in Naperville.

In an incredible tale, an old man on my tour told me that he was born in Naperville in 1921. He said that his family lived in a "shack" on Hobson road about a mile east of Washington Street. He said that his little sister would sometimes flip and flop on the bed uncontrollably, all the while yelling in a voice that wasn't hers! And, he said, they would often see a Phantom-like thing near her while it was happening! He said that his parents finally got fed up with it and moved from Naperville - to Detroit - and his sister never again had a fit, nor did they ever again see the entity.

A young woman (about 25) on my tour told me that she and a friend often see the Phantom in her bedroom when they use their Ouija Board! (By the way, the Ouija is a very bad idea. I have heard soooo many horror stories surrounding it. If you own one, do yourself a favor and throw it away. *Now*).

Back in 2009, my tour group was in Naperville's Central Park on Washington Street, I had just told them the story of the Phantom. The group was ghost hunting a bit before we moved on to the next location. It was then that I noticed a group of five women, from the tour, off to the side of the group, and they appeared to be upset at each other. I walked up to them and asked if there was anything I could do to help. One of the women spoke up, saying, "We're all sisters, we grew up here in Naperville, as did our parents and grandparents - and all five of us still live here with our own families. And get this: all of us have had that Phantom thing in our homes! All of us!" I couldn't believe it, I said, "I know the Phantom is all over Naperville, but I've never heard of it 'stalking' a family!" The lady said, "That's nothing, our parents used to talk about seeing a Phantom-like thing in their house! And so did our grandparents!" I said, "So you've got three generations of family who have had encounters with the Phantom here in

Naperville?" The woman just shook her head, yes. All five of the ladies were seriously upset.

Why would the Phantom be so interested in this one family line? Is there a connection? More on this later...

I have heard many more Phantom tales. They take place in all areas of Naperville: the historic area, new subdivisions, indoors and out. The Phantom is spotted in every corner of Naperville, nowhere is safe. But, from my experience, there is one place that seems to have more "Phantom activity" than any other single place in Naperville - Central Park. I have had people relate to me stories of Phantom encounters that occur in Central Park more than any other place!

Why Naperville's Central Park...?

Think about it: why would the Phantom spend so much time in Central Park? Also, on my tours participants have captured photos of our cloaked Phantom friend in the park on many occasions. Here's a photo of him, captured on my tour by a tour participant in 2010. The person saw something moving in the darkness and took the photo. In order to see the Phantom, who is black, in the darkness, we have had to overexpose the photo. But, by doing so, you can clearly see the Phantom in the background (inside the white circle).

Notice that he looks exactly has he has been described by previous witnesses – a "cloaked figure."

In addition, incredible amounts of spirit activity "kick up" in the park when I start to talk about the Phantom. Check out these photos of Orb

Showers that have occur when I talk about the Phantom while in the park:

HauntedNaperville.com

All types of spirit anomalies have been captured on photos in the park during our tours. There have also been white clouds in photos, mists along the ground, streaks of light as long as 15 feet, and much more. Why is there so much spirit activity in Central Park? And especially the Phantom activity?

Those are huge questions. But you'll be happy to learn that I've figured it out. I know who the Phantom is. And I know why he torments the people of Naperville.

It's not a pretty story, but here it is...

HauntedNaperville.com

The True Story of Naperville's Phantom

There are a few components to this tale, so let's start with why he's in the park so much. It helps to know a bit about the history of the park. First, Central Park wasn't always called Central Park. It was Naperville's first park and it was called The Town Square in the 1800s. It was a happy place. It was where all the town's activities happened. The big summer picnics, band concerts, ice skating in the winter, etc. There is even, to this day, an actual Civil War cannon in the park. Back in the old days, they would fire the cannon on 4th of July.

This is the Civil War cannon, in Central Park.
The wood base has long since rotted, to be replaced by cement.

Also in the park back then was the Dupage Courthouse building. You see, back then Naperville was the county seat for Dupage County. Today, Wheaton is the DuPage County seat. But, at one time, Naperville was (but that's another story...!)

When Naperville became the county seat back on June 17th, 1839, $5,000 was subscribed to build a county courthouse. The city fathers built it on the south side of the park (the area that today is behind the old Nichols Library.) Here's how it looked:

The DuPage County Courthouse, as it sat in the mid 1800s, in Naperville's Public Square (currently Central Park.)

The courthouse stood on a high stone foundation, with the county jail enclosed in the foundation walls. Research shows that the jail door was on the exterior of the building. In the door was a diamond-shaped cutout, at eye level, that allowed whoever was in the cell to look out on the park. The fact that the city jail was at one time in the park plays into the frequent appearances of the Phantom. Equally important is the fact that the incarcerated individual could look out on the park grounds. This is the first piece of our puzzle, now let's move on to the second piece...

It's Showtime...

In Naperville's historic business district, on Jefferson Street, midway between Main Street and Washington Street, is a building that looks like this:

You may recognize this building as the haunted theater building discussed earlier in this book. The building has quite a bit of strange spirit activity going on inside of it, as laid out earlier. But I'd like to relate now another event that occurred inside this building, an event not discussed in the Haunted Theater section of this book:

Back in April of 2008,
I was the Lead Investigator of a paranormal investigation
into this place.
And what we found has changed Naperville history.

There was a thunderstorm that night - for a ghost hunter it doesn't get much better than that! I met my team at the building. We were allowed overnight access to the ground floor and the basement. A few investigators were assigned places and duties on the ground floor. These duties included infrared video recording and photography. I continued into the basement with a psychic in tow. The psychic is a very talented young lady. She's been part of many of our investigations and has proven talented and invaluable.

She and I entered the basement. It was dark down there. It was quiet down there. Maybe *too quiet.*

She was walking around trying to get a read on the place. I was a few yards away from her with an EMF meter, taking readings and looking for "spikes" in the electromagnetic fields. All seemed very normal. Then...

The psychic, who was off in on of the basement corners, began to scream out saying, "You can't hurt me! You can't hurt me! You can't! You can't hurt me!"
I ran up to her and yelled, "What is it? What do you see?"
She pushed me back, screaming, "Get back, I can't protect you from it!"
I yelled, "Tell me what you see!"
She said, "Get back!"
I looked her in the eye and assertively said, "I'm the Lead Investigator, tell me what you see. *NOW.*"

She looked up at the wall, her eyes wide open as if she couldn't believe what she was seeing. She was obviously very shaken. Speaking to me, without looking at me, she said, "It's like black smoke. *Very dark.*"
I couldn't believe my ears -- she was looking at the Phantom! (This girl knew nothing of Naperville's Phantom, we'd never discussed it). I asked, "You are looking at black smoke right now? You're sure?" She continued staring at the wall and nodded '*yes.*' Mind you, this girl is very experienced in this sort of thing, she has seen everything – and yet, whatever she was seeing along that wall was scaring the hell out of her.

My opinion was that she was looking at the Phantom, so I said to her, "Quick, ask its name!"
She turned to me with a puzzled look and said, "What?"
I said, "Hurry, do it! Ask its name!"

She shook her head in befuddlement and turn back toward the wall and started screaming, "Who are you? Who are you? Who are you?" She only got it out about three times when she turned back toward me, bent over, on the verge of throwing up – she had like dry heaves.

I leaned down to her and said, "Would you quit throwing up and tell me what you see!!"

She looked at me and screamed, "It's trying to scare me, it just morphed into a hanging man!" And with that it was gone.

As we spoke about this a few minutes later, she told me that the hanging man was so grotesque that she practically threw up when she saw it!

I prepared a report on the findings of the investigation. In the report I wrote, "As far as I can tell, the Phantom, who has been terrorizing Naperville for 100 years, was in your basement. He was visible to my psychic in the southwest corner of the building. He tried to scare her by morphing into a hanging man." That's what I wrote.

I was wrong.

I was *wrong*.

You see, as I studied and researched this situation, I came to realize that the Phantom wasn't trying to scare the psychic when he morphed into a hanging man! He was answering her question! -- *Who are you?*

Get this: in all of Naperville's bizarre history there is only one hanged man. *One.* And it's a hanging cloaked in mystery – a perfect intermingling of macabre and mayhem for the fostering of an angry and unrested spirit. Unfortunately, in order to move on to our third piece of this puzzle we're going to have to dig up one of Naperville's most hideous secrets. It's a piece of Naperville's past that "they" would prefer to keep buried.

In order to unravel the mystery of the Phantom, we'll need to dig, so dig we will...

Blood Money

Our third piece of the puzzle...

Naperville in the 1850s was in the throws of the lavish Victorian era. Opulence and wealth were the name of the game. People around here worked hard, and the wealthy played hard. Their homes were of classic design, with uncompromised workmanship and quality of material, the likes of which we can't buy today at any price. Peaceful picnics and strolls, fat cigars & oysters, pineapple brandy, and an occasional carnival act passing through town were what occupied the minds of Naperville's well-to-do.

And that is why the events of Monday afternoon October 26, 1853 rattled this quiet town. That's why the wealthy, the farmer, and the worker bees, all began peaking through their parlor curtains before they answered a knock at their front doors. On that day Naperville changed. On that day an act occurred, an act so horrific that it set in motion a series of situations that to this day baffle us, haunt us, and leave one of Naperville's greatest mysteries still without answer.

It all started in Warrenville, just north of Naperville. Two Irish immigrant brothers, by the last name of Tole, were working for the railroad and had received their pay, 60 dollars - a lot of money in 1853. So much money in fact that it proved to be an irresistible temptation as it drew the attention of another Irishman, his name was Patrick Doyle. As the Tole brothers entered a local tavern and began to celebrate their new-found-wealth with a few libations, Doyle kept an eye on them, waiting for his opportunity to part them from their cash.

When the Tole brothers later that day boarded a wagon headed for Chicago, Doyle noticed how drunk Patrick Tole was, and he quickly boarded the wagon with them, all the while assessing them, keeping an eye open for a chance at their loot. It didn't take long. Several minutes into the journey, when they were just north of Warrenville Station, Patrick Tole, who was exceedingly drunk, fell off the wagon - literally. The wagon stopped and Patrick's brother jumped down to help him back to his feet. As the sober brother was assisting his drunken brother, the sober brother made a grave mistake – *he turned his back on Doyle.*

This was the opportunity Doyle was waiting for, and he grabbed it with fervor you might say. Witnesses say that while the Tole brothers were distracted, Doyle jumped down from the wagon, picked up a near-by fence post and proceeded to mercilessly beat the sober Tole until, witnesses said, his head broke open and spilled out into the mud. Doyle quickly went through the Tole brother's pockets, securing the 60 dollars and a small pocketbook, he quickly ran toward the train out of town.

Curious at this point is the fact that the pocketbook, with the money inside, was found just 20 feet from the bloody homicide scene. Did Doyle panic, drop the money, and not realize it? Did he realize he dropped it, but in his panic not want to waste the five seconds of precious escape time to pick it up? Or maybe, realizing the horrible act he'd just committed, did he throw the money on the ground, feeling it was the epitome of blood money, cursed even, he didn't even want it? We'll never know.

The wagon driver quickly road into Naperville and proceeded to the courthouse in Naperville's Public Square (currently Central Park.) There, he notified the sheriff (then, Naperville Sheriff Amos Graves) what had happened and gave him a description of Doyle. Meanwhile Doyle boarded a train for Chicago.

The next day the Chicago Police had Doyle's description, and two days later, on Thursday, while walking on Randolph Street, Doyle was arrested in Chicago. By Friday afternoon he was in the DuPage courthouse jail here in Naperville.

He had no counsel of his own, so local big shot attorney R. N. Murray was appointed to defend him. (This is the same R. N. Murray who hosted Stephan Douglas in his home on Main Street while Abraham Lincoln slept in the Pre-emption house, during the Lincoln-Douglas debates). The Doyle trial was set for the next term of the circuit court, a few months forward in the spring of 1854. Doyle sat in the courthouse jail (in Central Park) until the spring of 1854.

We don't know too much about the trial itself; there are no surviving records - they seem to have vanished into thin air! We do know we know from the newspapers of the day. Such as: Doyle was about 23 years old, slight build, tall, he was found guilty of the "willful murder of Patrick Tole" and became the first and only man officially hanged in Naperville as the DuPage County seat. (At the time, Naperville considered this their first execution. However, since Naperville lost the position of County Seat for DuPage before another major crime took place, it became their only execution).

Doyle was hanged about a mile east of downtown, on Chicago Ave. (The spot that was Ritzer's Gravel Pit). According to an eye-witness in attendance, the entire area was covered with people, out to witness the spectacle.

The speed with which this situation was handled speaks volumes as it pertains to how quickly the people of Naperville wanted to put it behind them and get back to their quiet lives. But the truth was that Naperville was now a different place - they had their first murder and execution, and there was no going back to the "good old days."

Now you would think that this would be the end of old Patrick Doyle. But as it turns out, *it's only the beginning...*

HauntedNaperville.com

The Plot Thickens

It seems the Saga of Murderer Doyle doesn't end on this piece of ground where the gallows were erected, or should I say three feet above this piece of ground. No, it continues to this day.

You see, Doyle was cut down, and, because he was Irish Catholic, his remains and coffin were brought to Naperville's Sts. Peter & Paul Cemetery for burial. Unfortunately, the Catholic cemetery officials refused to have a murderer interred in their sacred ground. OK.

Not to be deterred, they brought Doyle over to the new Naperville Cemetery on Washington Street. Unfortunately they were met with a similar situation - no place for Doyle. The officials at The Naperville Cemetery apparently had no problem with Doyle's murderous actions per se', it was *where* to put him that presented the problem - At that time, 1854, the cemetery didn't have a Potters field for burials of the indigent. Today the Naperville Cemetery is quite large, but back in 1854 the cemetery was only a few years old, and was composed of just the couple original acres of property donated by George Martin (along Washington Street.)

The officials at the Naperville Cemetery didn't leave the coffin-toters entirely without a solution however - they told them that if they would like to, they could leave the coffin in the back of the cemetery, unburied. And that's what they did! It's hard to imagine what their logic was, but they reasoned that leaving him unburied was an acceptable solution! (Perhaps they thought, '*he's a filthy murderer, the hell with him*'!) In any case, that's where the remains of Naperville's first execution ended up - unburied in the back of the cemetery.

Unfortunately, because it wasn't an actual solution to their problem, as time passed it only created more problems. Within days, the city fathers got wind of a plan that some medical students were going to robber the cadaver and use it for experiments! Quickly the coffin was retrieved before the students could commit their vile act.

Now imagine the scene: the city fathers of Naperville are standing around the coffin of their first execution and they have a huge dilemma – *they have nowhere to go with him.* One of the city fathers present at the meeting was a successful Naperville businessman named Phillip Beckman (he owned Beckman's Harness Shop, then located on the corner of Jackson Street and Washington.) Mr. Beckman offered the following solution to the others, "Why don't we simply put Doyle in the attic of the harness shop until we figure out a more suitable alternative. He'll be safe there." That offer was more than acceptable to the others, so, up into the harness shop attic Doyle went.

When Beckman retired, 40 years later, in 1893, Doyle's coffin and remains were discovered *still in the attic of the harness shop!* – they had been up there for almost 40 years! The harness shop, by the way, sat on land that today is home to Jimmy's Grill in downtown Naperville. (Note: The current building occupied by Jimmy's Grill is NOT the harness shop building, it only sits on the original land. The original Beckman's Harness Shop building was razed in 1946. After that, a gas station occupied the land, then in the early 1970s the current structure was built – originally a piano store).

When Beckman retired in 1893 and the coffin was discovered, a prestigious Naperville doctor named Hamilton Daniels claimed it and brought it to his office. (Dr. Daniels had an office on Washington Street that today would be located right across Washington Street from the old Nichols Library).

Dr. Hamilton Daniels

Once safe in his office, Dr. Daniels opened the coffin and discovered that Doyle was now merely a skeleton. The doctor kept it in a backroom of his office. When he retired in 1895, the doctor felt that the college could make good use the skeleton for anatomy classes, so he donated it to the college. A zoology student from the college remembers it being in use as late as 1914. But here's the problem now: *The college no longer has Doyle's skeleton and there are no records of it being disposed-of or properly buried.*

*So where are the bones of
Naperville's one and only execution?*

Did someone steal them for the history of it? In that case, is the skeleton in a Naperville basement, attic, or closet? Or maybe it was dismantled and used for various other demonstrations? Someone must know - skeletons don't just walk away. *Or do they?*

HauntedNaperville.com

Tying it All Together...

Getting to the bottom of the Phantom's identity began to come together when he appeared to my psychic back in April of 2008. He was visible to her in the basement of the old theater building on Jefferson Street. He took the form of thick black smoke. I have spoken to many people who claim to have encountered Phantom - all of them mention the fact that when he was standing still, he appeared as thick black smoke that undulated (when he moves he appears to be wearing a cloak or cape of some sort.) So it certainly seems that my psychic was "face to face," if you will, with the same smoky entity that so many Napervillians have experienced over the years.

At one point my psychic asked the Phantom who he was; she asked, "Who are you? Who are you?" Within seconds, he morphed into what appeared to be an executed, hanging, man. He was literally dangling from a noose; his head twisted around; his face repulsive to the point that she was on the verge of throwing up. My psychic quickly concluded that he was trying to scare her by morphing into something so hideous. It was only after some research (and a bit of ghost hunter intuition) that I came to realize that he wasn't trying to scare her, he was answering the question - Who are you?

He was telling us that he was a hanged man. Fortunately, Naperville has only one hanged man: Patrick Doyle. And, as it turns out, Doyle's story is ripe with mystery, madness, and mayhem. He has reasons for becoming the Phantom, lingering in Naperville, and terrorizing the town.

Point 1) Doyle's Court Trial Records are Missing.

It seems strange, that in a town like Naperville where such meticulous records have been kept regarding practically every aspect of our history, that all the courtroom records for the *one and only* execution in our town's history, are *missing*. One would think that these are important historic records and that they'd be protected. Instead, swoosh... they have mysteriously vanished into thin air. Is it possible that there is something in those records that those in 1854 didn't want us in 2012 to know? Is it possible that Doyle will continue to haunt Naperville until the truth of what happened in that courtroom is made known to all?

Because of the lost trial records, we don't know what evidence was presented against him. We also have no way of evaluating if he was properly represented and received a fair trial. We don't even know if the sheriff hanged the right guy! I have a feeling that something about that trial is amiss, and until we know the truth of what happened in that courthouse, we will never rid ourselves of our Phantom friend.

Point 2) The Phantom Haunts Central Park.

There are more cases of the Phantom haunting Central Park than anywhere else he haunts, that I know of. This situation gives us a major connection between the Phantom and Doyle. Why would the Phantom be in Central Park so much? If the Phantom is Doyle, perhaps he's in the park because when he was alive he sat in the courthouse jail looking out on the park, through the jail door window, for six long months. Did he perhaps develop a fondness for the park? Maybe, as a spirit, Central Park is the place the Phantom finds comfort in, and he spends much time there.

Point 3) It Appears Doyle Has Never Been Laid to Rest

With the debacle of Doyle's burial and the refusal of the town to properly lay Doyle to rest, is it any wonder that he is an angry and unrested entity? Doyle doesn't rest in peace because he was probably never respectfully laid to rest! This is a common situation with ghosts: we hear about homes being built on graveyards and many strange things going on in the home because the graves are not at rest. Once things are "made right" the spirit activity quiets down. But how do we make things right with Doyle?

Point 4) Doyle's Remains have Been Inhumanly Mistreated.

Spirits do not take kindly to the mistreatment of their bodily remains. Does Doyle seek revenge, from beyond the grave, for the horrific treatment of his remains? (For example: letting them sit unburied in a harness shop attic for 40 years!)

This evidence is especially powerful when the gross and inhumane treatment of Doyle's bones are considered. We know that mystically bones are *very powerful*:

Bones are used in Shaman rituals and incantations. Shaman wear human bones as jewelry, amulets, charms, and clothing. They wave bones in the air and pierce their ears and/or nose with them.

Witches use bone in spells, curses, rituals, and potions.

Organized religion uses bones! Do you know the difference between a church and cathedral? A cathedral has a small piece of saint bone in the altar. That's the difference! - *A piece of human bone.*

Back in Victorian America, wealthy people would purchase actual ancient Egyptian mummies and bring them home to America. Once here they would grind up the mummy (bones and all) and mix it in a glass with milk and drink it for the mystical "qualities" it produced. That's right, they got high by ingesting the human bones of ancient Egyptians! (Kind of a "Phar-oh-Val-tine". Lol.)

The power of bones to produce supernatural power is a well-accepted truth. Could Doyle, by the power of his unrested bones, be wreaking havoc in Naperville to this day? I believe that Doyle has a grudge against Naperville for the mistreatment of his remains, and for the possible miscarriage of justice that was his trial and execution. I believe that if he is guilty of the crime he was executed for, he certainly has it in him to be an evil spirit that terrorizes from beyond the grave.

Point 5) There is a Solid Connection Between Phantom and Doyle.

You may remember a few pages back I told you about five sisters on my tour who told me that all five of them had been paid visits from the Phantom. In addition, they told me that their parents had encounters with the Phantom, as did their Grandparents! The entire family line had had encounters with the Phantom in Naperville.

This seemed incredible to me, I had never heard of the Phantom "stalking" an entire family – one family member at a time! I asked those ladies, "Why would the Phantom be so interested in your family?" One of the sisters cleared her throat, and answered, "It might be because our family has been in Naperville for over 100 years, and our family name is *Doyle*!" I gasped, "Your family might be related to him!" The woman nodded, saying, "That's what we're thinking too."

So here we have a family named Doyle being "stalked" by the Phantom. Is it just a coincidence that he chose a family named Doyle? Or, is Patrick Doyle Naperville's Phantom?

In a story relating to the Phantom...

The Saints Peter & Paul Church Fire of 1922

Naperville has had a large German / Catholic presence from its beginning. Many of the original school classes, including the College, were taught only in German. The Catholic faithful have been aggressive in their establishment of both a parochial school in Naperville as well as a large edifice in which the faithful could gather together for worship.

There have been three Catholic Church buildings serving the parish in the historic area of Naperville. The original Catholic Church in this section of town was Saint Rapheal Church. It was a boxy, though functional, structure that was built by 25 pioneer families in 1846 (about 15 years after the founding of the town.)

St. Rapheal Church, circa 1855.

It was located a half block north of the current Sts. Peter and Paul church, on the Southeast corner where Franklin Street and Front Street intersect. (Front Street has since had its name changed to Ellsworth). Saint Rapheal Church was used until 1860. It was replaced as the house of worship when the first Sts. Peter and Paul Church was built on the Northeast corner of Ellsworth Street and Benton.

The original Sts. Peter and Paul Church

The first Sts. Peter and Paul Church was used faithfully until tragedy struck – On June 4th, 1922, Pentecost Sunday, the grand church burned to the ground. The parish was devastated. The photos below show the original Sts. Peter and Paul Church and the structure as it burned.

The Original Sts. Peter & Paul Church

Not to be defeated, the faithful set up temporary services in the near-by college structure Wenker Hall (Wenker Hall is named after Fr. Wenker, a parish priest instrumental in the building of the church, college, parochial school, and parish overall). They raised funds and hired Architect Hermann Gaul to design a new church - a church of brick and stone; a church that beckoned the faithful from every corner on Naperville with a steeple that reached over 200 feet into the sky; a church of classic Prairie Gothic design; a church *for the ages*. Mr. Gaul designed the current mesmerizing structure.

The new church construction was begun in May of 1925. Almost three years later the completed church was dedicated. Note: The cost of construction was over $300,000.00 in 1925 dollars. -- *At a time when there were only 350 families in Naperville's Saints Peter and Paul parish!*

Now let's step backward and revisit the fire...

When the original Saints Peter and Paul church burned in 1922 it created a Naperville mystery that to this day remains largely unsolved. The mystery? *What caused and fed the blaze?*

When speaking to old Napervillians about the church burning, it's not unusual for them to speak in hushed whispers and confide, "Everyone knows the KKK burned it down." Interesting theory but I disagree.

This fire was unique, *supernatural* perhaps. First of all the fire started in the only place in the basement where the flames could reach the roof so quickly, in other words: in the *worst possible place.* Yet there is no way it could have started there, there was nothing there to ignite a flame. Second, the fire burned so hot and so ferociously that *everything was destroyed* - paintings, furniture, glass, even the *statuary was destroyed. Everything.* Let me ask you: Since when does *stone statuary* burn? What could have possibly been feeding these ferocious flames?

An investigation into the fire at the time ruled the cause of the blaze "Undetermined Cause." This means officials were unable to determine how the fire started, or why it burned so hot and so complete. This wasn't the arson work of the KKK or a freak accident, if so the ignition process would have been clear to the investigators. No - *another force was at work here.*

Consider also, if you will, that there is a witness who claims that a *large black shadowy figure* was seen behind the church moments before the blaze erupted. -- A large black shadowy figure? Where have we heard that description before?

So, am I suggesting that the Phantom, who has been seen around Naperville for a hundred years, is responsible for burning Saint's Peter and Paul Church to the ground? You bet. Here's why:

This fire can't be explained. Investigators, even to this day, have been unable to determine how this fire started or what fed the flames to burn so ferociously and completely. Something supernatural may have been at work.

A witness claims that a large shadowy figure was seen behind the church a moment before the blaze erupted. A large shadowy figure is also something supernatural. This testimony places the Phantom at the church - *at the time the fire ignited.*

Of course, if we're going to go down this road – the road that asserts that the Phantom is responsible for the church burning, the question we must address first is WHY? Why would the Phantom bother? "Motive" is a key point in any crime; does the Phantom have a motive for such an action?

As I've studied the Phantom, and come to learn who he is and why he's in Naperville, I discovered that he *has* a substantial grudge against the Saint's Peter and Paul church! A grudge *so angry* that he could feel *completely justified* reducing the Saint's Peter and Paul Church building to a *smoldering heap!* He has a motive.

Let's go back to his execution...

You'll remember that he was hanged, then cut down, and placed in a coffin. Then, because he was Irish Catholic, he was brought - *where?* -To Sts. Peter and Paul Cemetery. And what happened there? Denial. He was denied the burial of his faith by the powers-that-be at Sts. Peter and Paul! And this denial to be buried in their cemetery is the reason he was never properly laid to rest *at all!* He was bounced all over town; rotted away in an attic; disgraced; mistreated; hung in a school classroom; and eventually completely lost forever, all because Sts. Peter and Paul denied him a proper burial.

Is he pissed at them? Pissed enough to burn their church down if he could? I say, *yep.*

HauntedNaperville.com

HauntedNaperville.com

Naperville Ghosts

Calling Dr. Ghostly...

Washington Street can get really dark near the Naperville Cemetery, especially in the wee hours of morning when there's no one else around. To some, it's at its darkest when the only illumination is the ghostly vision of a figure in a white robe wandering lost in the night...

Over the years there have been reports by drivers on Washington Street that a figure, dressed in a white robe, was seen just south of the cemetery, moving southward toward Edward Hospital. As the car gets closer, the apparition slowly vanishes.

Washington St., at Cemetery, looking south toward Hospital. A figure in white has been seen in this area.

The accepted theory is that the figure must be a restless spirit from the cemetery. A spirit that, for a reason or reasons unknown to us, periodically roams darkened Washington Street lost and bewildered.

I have a different theory.

It may be possible that the spirit is looking for the building it had dedicated its life to - a building that no longer stands. The building it was in when it took its own life... many, many, years ago...

To understand this haunt, it helps to know that the award winning Edward Hospital that stands on Washington Street, just south of the Naperville Cemetery, was at one time not a hospital at all, but a Tuberculosis Sanitarium.

Back in the early 20th century, the treatment for the life threatening illness Tuberculosis, or TB (also referred to as Consumption) was to be quarantined. The patient needed bed rest, fresh air, and lots of quiet if they were to make a recovery. Naperville's Edward Sanitarium, being surrounded by lush, peaceful, and spacious grounds, helped many people stricken with the illness to recover quickly.

Although the sanitarium was designed to provide help to those of modest means, the superior care provided by the sanitarium staff was known far and wide as the best available, as well as becoming a model center for others built around the country.

The treatment in Naperville was so effective in fact, that there is a story told that a very famous Hollywood movie star sought treatment here in Naperville's Sanitarium back in the 1940s. (I've been unable so far to secure a name. Being that the star wished privacy, there are no published records or news stories of the star's treatment here, just tales passed down).

The Sanitarium was originally built in 1907, a gift from Eudora Gaylord Spalding. When it was built, it was called the Chicago Municipal Tuberculosis Sanitarium. It was one of the first Tuberculosis treatment centers in the Midwest. At its helm was an imminent TB physician from Russia named Dr. Theodore Sachs. The facility quickly grew from its original 14 beds to well over 100.

The Sanitarium, under the direction of Dr. Sachs, began, from its inception, to ruffle feathers. At the time of its opening the prevailing thought was that the treatment of TB had to be done in a dry climate, particularly the southwestern climate. Dr. Sachs disagreed and proceeded to achieve impressive results in the moist Midwest air. He felt that TB could be treated in virtually any climate as long as proper rest, medications, hygiene, and diet were properly administered.

In 1920 a fire destroyed a good portion of the building. $150,000 was allocated, and a new building was erected and was renamed the Edward Sanitarium. That building served the patients until it also burned down, in 1955. By this time however, TB had become more easily treatable, and the Edward Sanitarium was rebuilt as a full-fledged hospital - Edward Hospital.

So how does this factor into the ghostly figure seen on Washington Street?

Back in 1916, Dr. Sachs had been expertly running the sanitarium for 10 years, but not without controversy. For years, Dr. Sachs had been hassled by Chicago politicians and governing bodies that sought to have him removed from his position. When their traditional tactics failed to generate the response they required, they brought out the big guns - they began accusing Dr. Sachs of mismanagement, and began belittling the sanitarium, his work, and accomplishments.

This went on for several years. Then, on Saturday, April 2, 1915, Dr. Sachs arrived at the sanitarium at his normal time: 6:30 p.m. He made his traditional rounds to the staff and patients. He then told his assistant that he would be resting in the sanitarium library.

Dr. Sachs

On the morning of Sunday, April 3, the lifeless body of Dr. Sachs was found on the library couch. Near him were two half empty bottles of medication. Tests showed them to be morphine and heroin. Beside the Doctor were two handwritten letters, one addressed to his wife, the other to the public. The public letter read:

"To the people of Chicago:

The Chicago Municipal Tuberculosis Sanitarium was built to be the glory of Chicago.

It was conceived in a boundless love of humanity and made possible by years of toil. No institution was ever planned more painstakingly or built more honestly. Every penny of the people's money is in the building, equipment, and organization.

The City of Chicago should make a most thorough inquiry into the entire history of the institution, and the community should resist any attempt of unscrupulous contractors to appropriate money which belongs to the sick and the poor.

Unscrupulous politicians should be thwarted.

The institution should remain where it was built, unsoiled by graft and politics, the heritage of the people.

In the course of time every man and woman in Chicago will know how Dr. Sachs loved Chicago and how he has given his live to it.

My death has little to do with the present controversy. I would not dignify it.

I am simply weary.

With love to all, Theodore B. Sachs"

Naperville was shocked by the news. Dr. Sachs had always placed the sanitarium and its patients first in his life, they knew that. He wholly dedicated his life to all things related to the sanitarium and the care of the patients. All of Naperville knew this to be fact.

The funeral, on April 5, 1915, was attended by thousands of friends, co-workers, neighbors, and colleagues. By order of the Naperville City Counsel, as a show of respect, all business in Naperville had to cease for the hour during the Doctor's interment.

Is the spirit of Washington Street the spirit of Dr. Sachs? I believe it is. There are several reasons why.

The first is that the Doctor was fiercely dedicated to the sanitarium. This type of attachment can easily cause a spirit to remain earthbound, in order to remain close to that which it holds so dear.

Another reason is that the Doctor was a Jewish suicide. Nowadays, Jewish suicides are not scorned; they are looked upon as mentally imbalanced and not spiritually responsible for their actions. This was not the case in 1915.

Jewish suicide was at that time a very shameful thing. The person who'd committed suicide was not permitted a full Jewish funeral. As well, the Shiva, a traditional seven-day mourning period, was not observed for the deceased. And, in most Jewish suicide cases, the Kaddish, a sacred prayer for the deceased, was not said.

The Jewish faith believed that when a Jew commits suicide, they are doomed to walk the earth. This is because the spirit cannot go back to the body because the body no longer functions. Furthermore, the spirit cannot move on its journey because its natural time has not yet come. This results in a very painful state of limbo for the Jewish suicide. Could the Doctor be doomed to walk the earth?

Many people feel that the spirit who walks Washington Street is a restless spirit who is buried in Naperville Cemetery. Actually, it's much *creepier than that.* You see, since Dr. Sachs was Jewish, he needed to be laid to rest in a Jewish cemetery. Unfortunately, because of his suicide, he wasn't welcome in the sacred ground of a Jewish cemetery. He also wasn't welcome in the Naperville Cemetery because it was a Christian burial place. In addition, he wasn't welcome at Saints Peter & Paul Cemetery, a Catholic burial ground.

So where is Dr. Sachs buried? Would you believe he was laid to rest in the ground of the sanitarium? That would be the grounds of Edward Hospital today!

Is it possible that the Doctor's spirit doesn't rest peacefully, either because of the suicide, or because he isn't resting in a Jewish cemetery? Is it possible that the Doctor is searching in vain for the sanitarium structure he loved so dearly - a building that no longer exists.

Is it possible that the Doctor is doomed to walk Naperville's Washington Street forever?

This investigation continues...

Update: I have come to learn that the ghost of a man is often seen roaming the hallways of Edward Hospital. The staff have taken to calling him Eddie (as in "Edward" Hospital), but I'd be willing to bet a more appropriate name would be Doctor Sachs...

HauntedNaperville.com

The Streets of Naperville

A Murderer Amongst Us

In Naperville's residential historic area are hundreds of homes built in the 1800s. Today, owners occupy these homes that share not only an appreciation for the craftsmanship quality, but the spectacular history that the homes contain as well.

Few homes in the historic area can lay claim to more prodigious history than the incredible French Provincial Mansion at 320 E. Chicago. The home was built by one of Naperville's most illustrious and generous residents - Professor James Nichols.

For his time, Professor Nichols was a giant among men. He was in the publishing business, and, in the late 1800s, he personally penned a book called: The Business Guide. The book offered its readers the Professor's invaluable wisdom and advice on such topics as: owning a business, making and saving money, investing, common sense for a quality living, etc. The book became a national bestseller, ultimately selling over four million copies! - A staggering number, especially in the late 1800s. In fact, in two of the years that the book was published it outsold the Bible!

The book made Professor Nichols very wealthy. And with some of that wealth he built the lavish estate at 320 Chicago Avenue.

Sadly, Professor Nichols died at 44 years old, in 1895. His widow and adult children continued to live in the house.

In the early 1900s the Professor's family were still very well off financially and this estate continued to be a Naperville showplace gem. The grounds were large and meticulously kept featuring formal gardens, a pergola, fruit trees, and a gazebo, all illuminated by flickering Japanese lanterns. The grounds also contained a large grape arbor so that two of the staff members

(Asian brothers named Haidu) could produce fresh wine right on the estate.

The estate also had other members of live-in servants as well, among them, a head maid, and a household supervisor named Mrs. Simpson.

At one point, the head maid proved exemplary. If fact, she so impressed Mrs. Simpson that she was given a promotion and a prime bedroom in the house – it was on the second floor and overlooked the beautiful back yard. One of the new duties entrusted to her with her promotion was the marketing for the family. This would entail purchasing the food, cloth, supplies, and such from the local merchants. Unfortunately, the temptation to "keep a few things for herself" proved too much and it soon became evident to her bosses that the young lady was "skimming" some of the product - she was promptly released from her duties by Mrs. Simpson.

A short while later, Mrs. Simpson learned that the head maid she had "sent packing" was arrested in Chicago for murdering her husband with an axe!

As the story would unfold, the Nichols family learned that the maid they had trusted with so much – who lived under their own roof - had viciously kill her husband, chopped his body into pieces, then packed the various parts into a steamer trunk, which she hid in her garage. Unfortunately for her, the sultry Chicago summer temperatures took their toll on the decomposing spouse bringing indescribable decay, pungently foul purification, and the interest of many hungry animals.

Some time later justice was served and for most people the young lady was all but forgotten - except by the occupants of 320 Chicago Avenue, in Naperville. You see, it took them awhile to get passed the overwhelming fear that someone capable of perpetrating such a horrific act had actually lived daily in their midst. The realization haunted them – *we could have just as easily been her victims under the right circumstances...*

HauntedNaperville.com

Naperville Ghosts

Haunted Horse Clops

They've been talked about in Naperville for over 100 years. Most people claim it to be simply haunted folklore. But, to the dozens of witnesses, this event couldn't get more *real*.

I refer to the Haunted Horse Clops of Naperville.

According to the legend, the streets that surround Saints Peter and Paul Catholic Church - namely Benton, School, Brainard, and Ellsworth - are home to a ghostly galloper that is on occasion heard but never actually seen! - A ghost *horse*.

The stories tend to be very similar: Usually in the wee morning hours, someone who lives on one of the mentioned streets is awakened by the sound of loud horse clops on the street outside their home. Curious who would have the nerve to ride a horse at such a ridiculous hour, they peer out their window to the street.

To their shock, the horse clops actually get louder as they pass by, and then gradually fade away down the street – but the stunned witness *never saw the horse*! This same spine-chilling scenario has played out countless times on the streets of Naperville over the last century!

There is a story told that claims that the horse isn't acting alone - there is a female rider on its back - a jilted bride. As the story goes, she was stood up at the altar of Saints Peter and Paul Church back in the mid 1800s. She rides her horse on the streets of Naperville, even to this day, waiting for the return of the man she was to wed.

Granted, this story has all the makings of a corny campfire frightfest, right down to the haunting heartbroken image of a jilted and scorned young lady. But is there anything valid here? *Could it be true?*

At this stage I do feel that the bride story is true. Our research has suggested that it most certainly *can be true*. But this isn't the time to address the bride, our focus for now is the horse clops themselves.

Is there a haunted horse of the streets of Naperville?

I'm happy to report that the horse clops *are actually happening*. Yes, we can prove it. In the early summer of 2011, one of our investigators, Chuck Kennedy (GhostsOfIllinois.com), was doing EVP recordings, overnight, on School Street, near the Ellsworth School. It was about 2am when he heard the faint sound of horse clops down the street! They were very faint, off to the east, but they seemed to be getting louder – as if the horse were heading west, getting closer to Chuck!

Chuck quickly secured his video camera. He engaged the record and then stood on the side of the street, and waited.

It only took a moment. The horse clops soon rang out very loud on the street as they passed by Chuck. And, just as with the other witnesses to the event, the clops faded away as the horse continued down the street. And, as with other witnesses, Chuck never saw a horse! In addition, the video camera didn't record a visual on the horse.

Thankfully however, the camera did record the sound of the horse clops!

This piece of incredible video evidence is historic, because it has moved the Haunted Horse Clops story of Naperville from "Folklore" to "Fact." All the witnesses over the years weren't crazy after all – they DID hear the horse clops. The haunted horse clops of Naperville ARE real, and we've got the video to prove it.

We aren't prepared to conclusively say that the bride is real too, not yet anyway. That investigation continues...

When people see the horse clop video, the first thing that hits them is how loud the clops are! That gives a lot of credence to the past witnesses who claimed that the clops were loud enough to wake them up.

But there is a disturbing aspect to this haunt as well...

Most ghost enthusiasts would classify the horse clops as an EVP, but that may not be true. You see, EVP is usually not heard with the human ear at the time it's communicated – it needs to be recorded and only becomes audible to the human ear on playback through a audio system. This is not the case with the horse clops – Chuck (and many, many, other witnesses) heard the horse clops *with their ears* in real time, *as it was actually happening!* The video camera also heard and recorded them. The horse clops are not a traditional EVP. The horse clops seem to be more like an actual ghostly haunt - *with sound!*

Very, very, strange...

Naperville Ghosts

Little Girl Lost

Imagine driving eastbound on 75th Street, between Book Road and Modaf Street. It is late night. The streets are relatively deserted. It is somewhat murky or misty outside, causing lights to take on an eerie, hazy, glow.

You've seen enough horror movies, in the back of your mind, perhaps even subconsciously; you're thinking 'perfect night to see a ghost...'

Indeed it is.

You see there are testimonies, as old as the late 1970s, from drivers on 75th Street who claim they've witnessed a young girl walking aimlessly along the shoulder of 75th Street's south side.

The witnesses claim that she turns toward their car, as if acknowledging it passing her. The headlights illuminate her small frame and pale face in the murky night air. She looks sad. The drivers can't believe there's a young girl, approximately 13 years old, wearing what appears to be pants and a loose shirt, out on the street by herself. In disbelief they look in the rearview mirror – sure enough, she is still there walking along the street.

The driver quickly stops and begins backing up the car to assist the girl, only to realize as they're backing up that she is no longer there!

They jump from their car to locate her – but she's *gone*. They look up and down the street, along the shoulder, some even call out to her hoping she'll respond – she doesn't. The street is quiet and hazy. Where did she go?

Naperville Ghosts

The Flower of Fort Hill
(or, the true story
of "Chicago Avenue Mary")

Looking east, from the corner of Washington Street and Chicago Avenue, the first thing you notice is that Chicago Avenue is a hill. What isn't readily evident is that the top of that simple unassuming hill is the most fertile story soil in all of Naperville. It is known as Fort Hill, and is part of what our ancestors called "the East Side."

This hill is where Indians danced around their fires. This is where Naperville implemented its defense during the Black Hawk War, its where the genius mind of Professor Nichols secured notoriety, its where the wealthy of Naperville hob knobbed. It's also where secrets were kept, and ghosts and murderers roamed with the area elite...

Stories of triumph and loss linger here. Tales of grand soirees and terminal illness creep through here. Solemn burial prayers and screams of murder echo here. Welcome to Naperville's Fort Hill....

When the Black Hawk war erupted in 1832, sending terror through the town, Joe Naper jumped to action. He assembled a group of men and soldiers to assist in the building of a fort, to use for protection. Running away, cowering, wasn't Joe Naper's style.

The group built their fort on the high ground of Chicago Avenue (then called Water Street.) They named it Fort Payne. It had a great view all around and a fresh water supply, compliments of a spring-fed pond on the south side of the hill's base. While building the fort, one of the group was killed by a marauding Indian, his name was Captain Paine. He was buried on Fort Hill, next to the fort. This, then, became the settlement's first burial ground. Many Indian dead, as well as pioneer dead, were buried right on the hill.

You may have noticed that the fort is named Payne and the officer killed was named Paine. Many conclude that the fort was named after the felled soldier; yet, this curious spelling has always been an interesting mystery. I have a theory.

I don't believe that the fort is named after the officer at all. Joseph Naper had a Reverend friend in Oswego, IL. When the settlement in Oswego received word of the Black Hawk plan to attack, most of the people of the town sought shelter elsewhere. Many stayed, standing firm, to fight for their town, among them Joe Naper's friend, the area's clergyman.

Unfortunately, their fight was in vain. The Black Hawk's attacked the Oswego settler's with a vengeance, mercilessly slaughtering them in the night - among the dead, Joe Naper's good friend, Reverend Payne. I believe Joe Naper may have named the fort in honor of his good friend, Reverend Payne, a forgotten hero of the war. It is, however, just a theory.

In 1836, several years after the war's end, Fort Payne was dismantled and a glorious mansion home was built for a wealthy pioneer family named Ellsworth. Louis Ellsworth purchased many acres of prime Naperville property, including Fort Hill. He named his estate Fort Hill (though some early Napervillians referred to it as Ellsworth Hill).

His mansion was a showpiece gem of DuPage County, complete with panoramic views of Naperville and the river, as well as a spectacular spring-fed pond in the "backyard." The Ellsworth Family was very charitable and civic minded, inside the Fort Hill estate, Mrs. Ellsworth operated one of Naperville's first schools.

They threw lavish parties entertaining friends, neighbors and business associates, among them a young lawyer named Abraham Lincoln. Here in this spectacular setting, Mr. and Mrs. Ellsworth raised their four children: Eva, Milton, Lewis Jr. and his twin sister, Carrie.

History books are filled with the incredible events that have unfolded on this simple plot of land known as Fort Hill. Yet there is one story - never told completely until now - a story so sad, so heart breaking, so unbelievable, it penetrates time and dimension...

The year was about 1947. A couple of students from the college were on a date in downtown Naperville. They had taken in dinner and a movie and were driving back to the college. They drove south on Washington Street and turned left, heading east up Chicago Avenue. When they reached the top of the hill, from out of nowhere, in the darkness, a young woman stepped out in front of their car.

The young woman turned her head, looking directly into the windshield. She made eye contact with the driver. Her eyes were wide open with the horrific realization that she was about to be hit. The man slammed on the brakes. His date screamed. They struck the young woman, and she disappeared beneath their car as it screeched to a halt.

The two panic-stricken youths leapt from the car to assist the girl. They looked under the car expecting a most macabre sight, but she wasn't there. They looked around the area: out on the street, up in the grass, but she was... *nowhere*. They couldn't understand it - they both *saw her* get struck. Perplexed and bewildered, they headed back to the college.

Over the next 45 or so years, there were many more appearances of the young woman. In fact, she'd become somewhat of a celebrity. The college students liked the idea of possibly "running into" her. And over the years, many, to their horror, *did*.

Although the encounters vary, the witnesses describe her basically the same way every time. The woman is about 24 years old, she's somewhat tall, has brown hair, and she wears an early American pioneer-type one-piece dress. Over the years, they'd given her names, such as: Chicago Avenue Mary, Gladys, and Brenda.

Gradually, she has become the stuff of legend with many sightings in various types of scenarios:

Most often she simply materializes in front of a stunned driver. A street lamp illuminates her pale complexion, her eyes large and shocked as the car slams its brakes and she disappears beneath it. The driver left harrowing, frightened, and confused in the dark.

Sometimes she's observed simply walking southbound down Ellsworth Ave. She crosses Chicago Avenue and continues over the hill into the night.

Sometimes people see a young lady sitting on the edge of the pond soaking her feet in the water – only to vanish in an instant before their shocked eyes.

Once, when students were relaxing at the bottom of the hill near the pond, they witnessed a young woman come over the hill. She was wearing a one-piece Civil War-era dress. She had a pale, stark, emotionless expression on her face. She stared off into the distance, unaware of the others on the hill. She moved along but didn't appear to be walking – just floating or gliding. Her lengthy brown hair and long dress were blowing in the wind. She moved over the hill, toward the pond, only to vanish slowly as she moved closer to them.

So is she just an urban legend? Did the college students make her up for attention – or after a few drinks? Could these stories be true? Can this ghostly young woman really exist?

This author is happy to say that this woman, the Flower of Fort Hill, definitely *does* exist. This young lady most certainly haunts this strip of street and Fort Hill. But who is she? And why is she here?

These stories have been part of Naperville folklore for many decades, and it gives this author great pleasure to finally disclose, for the first time in the history of Naperville, the actual identity of this woman and her reasons for haunting Fort Hill. Ladies and gentlemen, the Flower of Fort Hill...

Earlier we mentioned that back in 1836, a family named Ellsworth lived on the Fort Hill property and that there were four children, among them a daughter named Eva. Eva, being born in 1842, as a young lady in 1862, would have worn Civil War-era clothing similar to the clothing that the ghostly lady is wearing. In fact, their style of clothing would be identical.

Of course, just because they dress alike doesn't mean much. But, where the puzzle pieces fall into place is with the fact that Eva Ellsworth *died suddenly on September 15, 1867, at 25 years old –the same age as the specter that is seen!*

Eva died suddenly on Sept 15, 1867, at 25 years old, 140 years ago, wearing Civil War-era clothing!

Not only that, her home was on the same grounds that the ghostly girl roams! Eva died suddenly at a time in her life when she called these grounds "home." She would walk around the hill. The pond that the ghostly lady soaks her feet in was Eva's pond, in her backyard. We look at Fort Hill and see a public street and public grounds, but to Eva this is her home. Eva was very much attached to the home and family she loved, and she was taken away much too early. In fact, she's decided to stay around for a while.

The pond at the base of Fort Hill where Eva soaks her feet...

Of course, there's an obvious question: Why is Eva's spirit continually being hit by a car? Unfortunately, the history books don't tell us how Eva died. They simply say she "died suddenly." This author is going to conclude that a moving object such as a horse or carriage killed Eva. I believe the accident occurred at the exact spot where the cars are encountering her.

Eva's haunt plays out like she's being hit by the car, but the truth is: when Eva's eyes open wide and appear to make eye contact with the driver, Eva is not seeing the car or driver; she is seeing whatever struck and killed her back on September 15, 1867. In short, we are watching the last 20 seconds of her life play out over and over.

Why the last 20 seconds of her life? I believe Eva may have committed suicide by stepping in front of a quickly moving horse or carriage. Suicides often, though not always, remain earthbound. Since there was so much speculation on the suicide, I decided that the only one who can help us understand all this was Eva herself – I scheduled a séance on the grounds of Fort Hill for the anniversary of her death, September 15th, 1867...

Update:

A group of us gathered, about 10 in number, including a reporter from the Naperville Sun newspaper and a psychic. The date was September 15th, 2009. The evening was comfortably cool.

I didn't give the psychic any background on the situation, so as not to taint or influence the outcome. All I told her is that "we think a girl is haunting the grounds." We all sat down in the grass as the psychic sought to make contact.

Very quickly the psychic said, "There's a lady here with us." She asked out loud, into the air, "What is your name?" The psychic looked at me and said, "I think she said her name is Ellen."
I asked, "Could it be Eva instead of Ellen?"
The psychic asked for the name again, then she sighed, "Yes, it's Eva, not Ellen."

I asked, "Is she the girl who has been seen here who gets hit by the cars?" The psychic repeated the question to the spirit, then looked at me and said, "Eva says this is her place."

I said, "Ask her if she committed suicide here."

The psychic asked, "Eva, did you kill yourself here?" The psychic barely got the question out when she quickly reacted to Eva's response by yelling, "Whoa! Whoa! Holy crap!"

I yelled, "What!?"

The psychic, her eyes wide open reflecting her shock, said, "When I asked the question, Eva covered her ears and started yelling 'No! No! No!' *really loud*! I've never seen a spirit react like that before!"

I asked, "What do you think it means?"

The psychic answered, "She is obviously very upset by the question, which leads me to believe that it's true and it's something she regrets and doesn't want to address."

Eva communicated with us no more that night.

In 2011, I had the pleasure of working with two talented paranormal investigators named Beth Shields and Kristin Tillman. At the time, they worked with my investigation partner Chuck Kennedy and myself - we were called "HearAfter Research."

As part of our continuing efforts to understand the haunts of Naperville, the HearAfter Investigation Team went to the Naperville Cemetery to see if the ladies could communicate with Eva and perhaps convince her to tell us what happened on the night she died - September 15th, 1867.

It was a beautiful summer afternoon when we met up at the Ellsworth Family burial plot, in the Naperville Cemetery. The entire family is interred there, including Eva's parents as well as her two brothers and a sister.

It only took a moment to get our question answered! Oh, not by Eva - she was still silent on the subject - but, when the ladies posed the question to the graves, "We want to know, did Eva commit suicide or not?" The EVP digital recording registered a very clear male voice answering the question with the response, "She killed herself that night." We don't know if the voice was Eva's father or one of her brothers, as mention, all of them are interred in the spot where the EVP was captured.

It is great that we have solved the mystery of Eva's suicide – and we learned it from someone who was there that it *did happen*! Now, though, we need to find out how she killed herself. Our opinion is that she did it by stepping out onto the street in front of something that ran over her.

The intersection at Chicago & Ellsworth where Eva is struck

The hill over the pond where Eva has been seen

As we look westward, we can see how steep Chicago Avenue is at the spot where Eva's ghost is seen. History books tell us that this hill was extremely steep back in the 1800s, much more steep than today. So steep and muddy in fact, that in order to get to the top, a horse had to move at full gallop starting all the way west at the river! The horse had to be moving at considerable speed upon reaching the base of the hill if it was to have any hope of scaling it to the top.

This means that Eva, knowing that a horse (or horse and carriage) would be moving at a very fast pace as it reached the top of Fort Hill. If she chose to end her life, she could do it by stepping out in front of that fast moving vehicle as it reached the hilltop. This could be why Eva is continually "hit" by cars to this day – she is reliving the last few seconds of her life - right before her suicide.

We do know that as late as the 1930s, early automobiles had difficulty getting to the top of Chicago Avenue's hill. The hill today, although still steep, isn't anything like the mega-steep Fort Hill of old.

So we can finally set the record straight and stop suggesting that this haunt is a heartbroken lover with a vial of poison named Mary. Her name is Eva. Eva Ellsworth. Yes, Eva died suddenly, and it would seem that even in death, there were a few things that she won't let go of – like soaking her feet in her pond!

She truly is the Flower of Fort Hill.

Naperville Ghosts

Second-Act Sally

Tim seated himself comfortably in his seat at the Barbara Pfeiffer Auditorium, the playhouse theater on the grounds of North Central College. The performances here are always top notch; Tim had a feeling tonight's experience would be thrilling.

Even he could have never anticipated just how thrilling it would get...

The performance was in full swing as the lights came up, signaling the end of the first act in this evening's entertainment. Tim stretched in his chair as the patrons around him began to get up from their seats for the intermission. His eyes adjusted to the brighter light, and he decided that perhaps a cigarette and martini would be a nice addition to the evening. He still had time before the second act started.

Tim went out to the lobby, secured an extra-dry martini, lit his cigarette, and kicked back on an available chair. "This is living," he thought. His timing was perfect, just as he finished the cigarette, the lights flashed on and off, informing the guests that the show would resume in five minutes. He polished off the martini and headed back to his seat.

As he approached his seat, he could see that it was now occupied by what appeared to be an old woman in a blue dress. When he reached his row, it looked familiar. But perhaps the martini was clouding his memory - maybe this isn't where he was sitting previously. He rummaged through his pocket extracting his ticket, - seat G42 - then he checked the seat numbers. That <u>was</u> his seat. The woman was in the wrong place.

He stood for a moment, deciding how to evict the old woman. She looked up at him smiling, "Hello." Tim smiled and nodded, "Hello." She looked back toward the stage. Tim took a breath, and said, "Excuse me, you appear to be sitting in my seat." He showed her the ticket. She looked at it, and smiled, "I'm sorry, no, this is my seat."

Tim felt helpless. What now? Remove her bodily? He decided to let an usher handle it. He went to the lobby, and found a helpful young man on usher duty. He explained the situation, and the man followed Tim back to his seat. As they neared Tim's seat, it was clear to Tim that the woman was no longer there. The seat was empty. He turned to the usher, "Hey, she's gone."

Both men stood at Tim's empty seat. "She was here a minute ago," Tim apologized. The usher shrugged his shoulders, "She must have realized her error and left. Do you see her anywhere? I'll go make sure she's in the right place." Tim looked all around, "I don't see her anywhere. She's very old, white hair, a dark blue dress..." Both men looked up and down every row. She was *not there*.

Just then the lights dimmed. The usher looked back to Tim, "Enjoy the rest of the show, Sir."

Tim took his seat, seat G42, and didn't realize until several years later that he'd had an encounter with Second Act Sally, the most famous of all Pfeiffer Theater's... ghosts.

There have been many sightings of Sally over the years. Patrons as well as students have claimed to have either had an exchange with her, or they simply saw her sitting in her seat one moment – and then she was... *gone*. There have been many sightings of the old woman sitting in seat G42, and on occasion students, while rehearsing a play, will glace out into the darkened rows of seats and see an elderly woman watching the rehearsal, only to vanish slowly when she's discovered - refusing to heed her own final curtain call.

So who is she and why is she here? After investigation, this author has concluded that she may be a victim of a very common reason human spirits remain earthbound after their deaths – unfinished business. There are occasions in which a ghost has some task or project it started on earth that it desires to finish before it continues its spirit journey. It is a very common reason ghosts haunt.

Sally has appeared during many performances over the years, and her unfinished business is that she is waiting for the second act of a show she started many, many, years ago...

The Barbara Pfeiffer Theater

It was March of 1966 when a young playwright named Robert Lewis, was debuting his first musical at Naperville's Pfeiffer Hall. Mr. Lewis was not an unknown author. He'd enjoyed previous literary success - he'd written several TV scripts, including a few for the Alfred Hitchcock Hour in the late 1950s and early 1960s. He was very excited to be debuting his newest project, a musical version of Captain William Bligh's voyage on the H.M.S. Bounty and the mutiny that occurred aboard her. The play was called Bligh Me.

HauntedNaperville.com

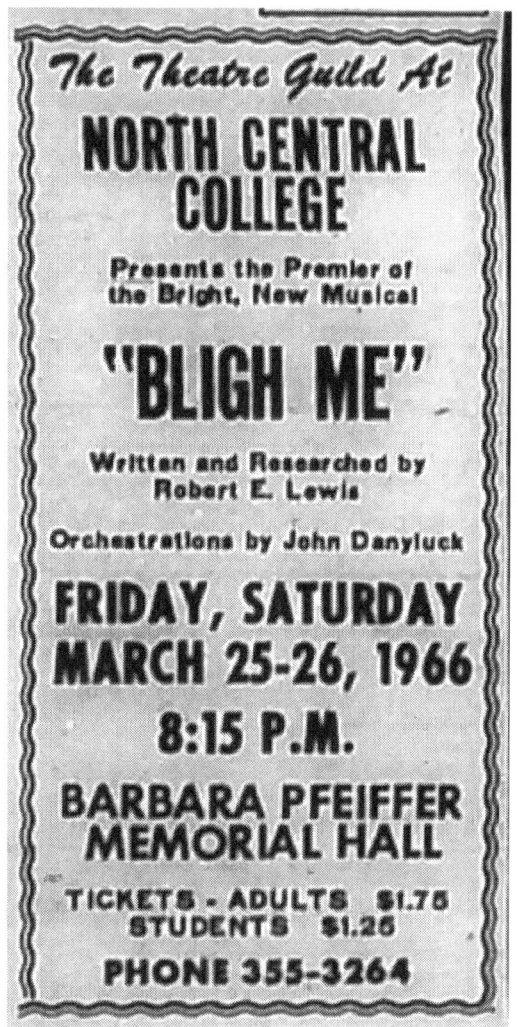

Actual newspaper ad for the performance of "Bligh Me."

Naperville didn't disappoint him; the whole town showed up to support one of their local boys who made good in Hollywood! The show completely sold out. Luckily, Mr. Lewis had reserved several seats for his family, among them, in seat G42, his elderly great aunt. This author refers to her as Sally.

According to a retired North Central professor who was in attendance that night, the lights dimmed, the music swelled, the curtain rose at exactly 8:15pm, and Sally peacefully joined the unliving. Several people seated around her, most likely family, thought she had only fainted. As the play started, they discreetly secured the assistance of Theater Professor Shanower, who was in charge of scenery and production that night. Realizing the severity of the situation, Professor Shanower quickly enlisted the services of noted Naperville physician, Dr. Glenn Wolf, who happened to be in attendance.

As the show continued, the two men lifted the unconscious woman out of her seat and brought her out into the lobby. As they lay her on a seat, it was obvious to the doctor that something was very wrong - the woman was no longer living.

Dr. Wolf immediately notified the local ambulance service of the distressing situation and waited for them in the lobby.

Unfortunately, as the first act was ending, the old woman was still not picked up. At any moment, the patrons would be released for intermission, and there was a deceased woman in the lobby.

The two men, thinking quickly, out of immense respect for the woman, gently moved her into the coatroom as intermission began. Of course, the play's attendees had no idea that someone had expired during the show and was now in the coatroom. Fifteen minutes later the crowds filed back to their seats just as the ambulance showed up and removed Sally to the morgue.

So what is Sally's unfinished business? I believe the key to understanding this haunt is in the timing of the evening's events. The truth is, Sally never saw the second half of her grand nephew's play, an event that was extremely important to her. As her remains lay in the lobby, she still enjoyed the show - granted, in a "ghostly state," *but she was there.* Unfortunately, when her body was moved to the morgue at the start of the 2nd act, she went with it, missing the second half of the play. After she'd been laid to rest, her spirit came back to the auditorium for the second half of the show, but it wasn't there. So she continues coming back. And she'll continue to do so because she has unfinished business – seeing the end of Robert's first musical play.

I should add that it is possible, too, that this haunt may be fed by guilt. You see, there is an old theater superstition: "If someone dies during the performance, this is a terrible omen for the play." Does Sally feel that her death during the performance is the reason the play's success never ventured outside the walls of Pfeiffer Hall?

Pfeiffer Hall has many spectacular performances all year long. If you have a chance, why not attend? You may have a chance meeting with an old woman looking in the dark for her seat - seat G42.

Authors note: It's hard to believe, but there is another musical version of Mutiny on the Bounty! Produced in 1985, written by rock star David Essex and Richard Crane. This is not the same production that Sally is waiting for.

HauntedNaperville.com

Naperville Ghosts

Upstairs / Downstairs

 Mr. Frederick Kailer built a large building at 216 S. Washington Street (east side, just south of Jefferson) back in 1897. The Kailer name still adorns the top front edge of the building. Mr. Kailer owned and operated the building, and the dry goods business inside it, for many years. He worked extremely long and hard hours inside those walls.

This building on Washington Street has been the location of a haunt. Several people are witnesses, on several occasions. The haunt that has been reported in this building is of a man, dapper and well dressed, in period clothing from perhaps the early 1900s. It is an interesting haunt in that it showcases an aspect of the paranormal that we generally wouldn't think about - that ghostly spirits can be indifferent to the physical aspects of our current time, and they operate in their own time and surroundings.

Here's what makes this haunt unique: The spirit is seen walking up a flight of stairs, inside the building, against the wall in the rear of the building. He appears to be simply walking up to the second floor. But get this - there are no stairs there!

The spirit is walking up a stairway that is no longer in that part of the building.

From what I understand, the stairway used to be there. The problem came when the second story of the building was converted to apartments. The tenants of the upstairs apartments had to enter the street level tenant's property and then use the interior rear stairway to get up to their apartments. To solve this problem, the original stairway was removed and relocated to a more convenient place for the upstairs tenants.

The ghostly visitor still uses the original stairway.

The one he used when he was living...

The Streets of Naperville

Step Right Up

"Step right up, you won't want to miss this…"

Jefferson Street is where the action is in Naperville. No doubt. But it hasn't always been that way. Back in the "very old days," the street to the south of Jefferson Street, currently Chicago Avenue, was named Water Street, and it was the heart of downtown Naperville. Jefferson was just a side street. As the city grew, spreading north, the center of town moved north too, making Jefferson Street the center of downtown Naperville.

The spectacular stone building with the arched windows, on the south side of Jefferson Street, at 18 West, has a long and varied history. It was built from locally quarried materials in 1891, at a cost of $6,656.08. It was Naperville's original bank. The city purchased it in 1917 and made it the City Hall and jail. It has always served its occupants well and been a jewel of downtown Naperville.

On occasion, in the evening after City Hall closed for the night, this section of Jefferson Street in front of City Hall was a "stage" for traveling shows passing through Naperville! Through the mid- 1900s many traveling freak shows, circuses, carnivals, and gypsy shows passed through Naperville. They stopped here on Jefferson Street to wow us, thrill us, fortune-tell us, and on occasion cheat us. (To get "gypped," comes from the word "gypsy").

Our city was very attractive to them. It was easy to get to - we had roads and rail. We were friendly; we were starved for entertainment; we had lots of people with disposable income; and our location was convenient - between two hot spots, Chicago and Aurora.

The original City Hall building on Jefferson Street.

In November of 1944, Eddie Polo, the original Superman from whom the comic book hero gets his name, performed his "thrill show" in Naperville. He amazed the gathered crowd when he broke iron chains with his bare hands and chest. The crowd reeled when he pulled a loaded truck along Jefferson Street, using only his hair!

His female companion, Superlady Sheila, also performed similar feats in the same show.

Fortune telling Gypsy shows complete with crystal ball, tarot cards, snakes, monkeys, wrestlers, boxers, and even live grizzly bears, would dazzle our ancestors with amazing feats of dexterity and magic – for a price.

These carnival and sideshow producers would search the globe to find the strangest acts imaginable. And many of them would make their way to Naperville. One of those shows is particularly interesting...

On April 14, 1865, a famous actor named John Wilkes Booth assassinated then-President Abraham Lincoln. Booth fled and eluded authorities for a couple days. He was eventually located held up in a barn in Virginia. He ultimately died outside that barn from gunshot wounds he received during the confrontation.

Fearing the body would be stolen from a public grave, he was buried in a secure prison cellar for safekeeping. Booth's family later moved the body to a secret, more dignified, location.

Some historians, however, claim that Booth was never actually apprehended and that a look-alike was killed in his place. In fact, reported sightings of John Wilkes Booth were filed for many years from the western frontiers of America to as far away as India.

One man in Enid, Oklahoma, calling himself John St. Helen, told many people in the bars he frequented that he was John Wilkes Booth, and that he'd gotten away with killing Abraham Lincoln. Then, one day in 1903, 38 years after the Lincoln assassination, in an Oklahoma boarding house, John St. Helen committed suicide by drinking wine laced with strychnine.

Of course, the suicide only fueled the fire of controversy surrounding his claim to be Booth. In an effort to quiet the speculation once and for all, a court, in 1931, allowed the exhumation and autopsy of John St. Helen. Six Chicago doctors performed tests on the body. Results would be analyzed and records compared, to prove once and for all that St. Helen was simply an unimportant man carrying a rouse to the bitter end.

If only it was that easy.

Tests were done and medical records compared. Curiously, many similarities to Booth were detected, including a striking photographic resemblance, being the same size and build, having a scarred right eyebrow, a crushed right thumb, as well as – hold on to your hats - a fractured heal of the same leg Booth injured in his escape from Fords Theater!

(In an interesting bit of irony, Booth tripped on the American flag that draped Lincoln's seating area, as he jumped over the edge to escape. He landed on the stage in a contorted fashion, fracturing his foot. Many believe it was this injury that kept him from fully executing his escape plans, and ultimately lead to his capture).

A carnival producer sniffed the opportunity and purchased the skeleton of John St. Helen! He then had it mummified and toured with it in macabre sideshow carnivals for years - claiming it to be the actual body of John Wilkes Booth! It would have most certainly stopped here because the attraction toured extensively in Lincoln's home state of Illinois.

In all likelihood, the show-spectacle of "The John Wilkes Booth Mummy" unfolded right here in front of our City Hall, as so many other Illinois traveling carnival shows had.

Note: One of the few men who would know if the man buried in the prison cellar was the real John Wilkes Booth was the man who actually killed him – Sergeant Corbett. Unfortunately, Sergeant Corbett committed suicide shortly after capturing and killing "Booth." Is it possible that Corbett was part of an elaborate government assassination cover-up that made him unable to live with himself?

The Street of Naperville

Coffins, Coffins, Everywhere

The building at 20 West Jefferson was at one time a pioneer undertaker, possibly Naperville's first.. At the time there was an alley along side the building and a barn in the back where coffins were made. From Jefferson Street you could look down the alleyway and see the coffins all laid out on the ground, standing up along the building, and even laid out on the sidewalk along Jefferson Street! What an eerie sight it must have been.

Once Lined with Coffins...

At the time this was happening, the mid 1800s, America's Victorian's weren't very concerned about death. In fact, death barely rated as a fear when a survey was taken in the late 1800s. The question on the survey was: What are you afraid of? From over 1,700 respondents, the most popular answer was Thunderstorms, followed by Reptiles at number 2, Stranglers at 3, Darkness at 4, and rounding out the top 5 fears was Premature Burial!

One might say that Victorians were so comfortable with death that they were entertained by it! The Victorians were quite the paranormal partiers. They'd throw raucous elaborate affairs and at the center of it all was the crystal ball. And of course there were tarot cards, mystery stories, ghost stories and the highlight of the evening – the séance!

During these parties they weren't shy about experimenting with unconventional recreational narcotics and hallucinogens. How unconventional? They were known to import ancient mummy from Egypt. They would them pulverize the mummy and grind it into powder. Then they would ingest it (eat it) for the magical qualities it possessed. Yeah, they got high on corpse.

All this macabre ritual made them quite at ease around death.

People of the time usually died in their homes, after a quick illness, surrounded by family and friends. It wasn't unusual for the corpse to stay in the home until burial - as many as four or five days. Often children in poor homes would have to share a room, or even a bed, with a dying or dead person.

Death was so common to children, one of the jump rope verses they would playfully shout was: "Grandmother, Grandmother tell me truth, how many years am I going to live? One, two, three, four...."

Even though the Victorian Napervillians were comfortable with death itself, they weren't comfortable at all with the idea of having a ghost in their house. Having a ghost in your house was considered a very bad thing and they had very strict guidelines for dealing with a death within their walls of their home - to avoid the possibility of ending up with a ghost inside.

Rule 1) When death comes, quickly cover all mirrors with a black cloth or turn them toward the wall. Because if the spirit sees itself in the mirror, it may get scared and decide to stay - then you've got a ghost.

Rule 2) When death comes, open the windows of the room in which a person had died, to let the spirit out freely. If the ghost can't get out of the room easily he may decide to stay – then you've got a ghost.

Rule 3) When death comes, quickly unlock all locks and untie all knots. If during its departure the spirit gets entangled in a knot or lock, he may have to stay – and you'll have a ghost.

Rule 4) When death comes, place a plate of salt in the room to purge the decease's sins. If your ghost is concerned about judgment for his sinful life, he may not want to proceed on his journey – then you've got a ghost.

Rule 5) Always carry the dead body from the home feet first, so the decease can't look back with regret and decide to stay – if he does, you've got a ghost.

And rule 6, the most important rule of all: Never, ever, ever allow a cat to be alone in a room with a corpse. The cat could be a demon and could turn your beloved corpse into a vampire...

HauntedNaperville.com

Naperville Ghosts

April 25, 1946 – 1:03 p.m.

In the heart of Naperville's historic residential area, where Loomis Street intersects the railroad tracks, there may be one of the most densely populated haunts in America.

It all began on April 25th, 1946. The Advance Flyer passenger train had just left Chicago on its way to Omaha. As it approached Naperville, it received a message claiming that a large blue flame was seen shooting out beneath the locomotive. The train came to a stop at the Loomis Street platform for an unscheduled inspection. The Exposition Flyer was on the same track just three minutes behind, nine cars long, traveling 85 miles an hour. The message was sent up the line informing the Exposition Flyer that the Advance Flyer had stopped --- *They didn't get the message.*

The engineer on the Exposition Flyer, Mr. Blain, didn't see the yellow or red warning lights, and by the time he came around the bend in the track, it was too late. Unable to stop, the engine of the Exposition Flyer tore into the last car of the Advance Flyer - ripping the final coach down the middle. Then it telescoped itself into the dining car, and the rest of the four cars were tossed off the track. It was 1:03 p.m.

Witnesses say the thunder of the crash roared through the countryside like a bomb. Then there was a tragic silence. ... Then the screams started.

Eyewitnesses reported seeing flesh and bone oozing from shattered windows. Thankfully, an off-duty Naperville policeman lived right down the block. He radioed for help and within minutes of the crash, doctors, nurses, ambulances, and hundreds of volunteers were racing to the scene from all the surrounding areas. Kroehler Furniture Manufacturing, located in the large brown building just north of the tracks, was a booming business in Naperville at the time. They sent all 800 employees to help with the rescue efforts.

HauntedNaperville.com

Haunted Train Track Crossing at 4th Ave. & Loomis

As they were removed from the wreckage, the dead and injured were laid out along 4th Avenue on the grass. As the hour approached 2:30, the concern shifted to the children of Naperville - they would be released from school and would witness the horrific scene. The dead and injured were quickly moved to area hospitals, Naperville funeral homes, and into the Kroehler Manufacturing building, converting it into a makeshift triage and morgue.

Ultimately, 44 people died in an instant, another a short time later in an Aurora hospital. Between 70 and 100 people were injured. Almost all of the dead were in the rear coach and dining car of the Advanced Flyer at the moment of impact. To this day, the Great Naperville Train Wreck still ranks as one of the worst train disasters in American history.

In the ensuing months, several investigations concluded that the engineer of the Exposition Flyer, Mr. Blain, was negligent in his duty. He was ultimately charged with manslaughter. The investigations concluded that the emergency brakes were never engaged, although Mr. Blain claims that he did engage them. Tests showed that if the brakes had been engaged, even after the second warning light was seen, the Exposition Flyer would have stopped over 900 feet from the Advance Flyer. Curiously, the larger and longer a train is, the easier it is to stop. Usually up to 15 cars long, on April 25th the Exposition Flyer had only nine cars.

To this day, passers-by along 4th Avenue where the collision occurred report strange happenings including apparitions that are walking along the street and vanish into thin air, shadow figures, large blue orbs in photographs, blurred photographs, cold drafts, strange noises, and more.

A ghostly mist captured at the haunted tracks.
Photo by James Hunter

A psychic was brought to the accident location without being given any background information of the crash. She walked up and down the block several times and then reported that there were dozens of confused spirits walking aimlessly around the street. Most of them, she concluded, were unaware they were dead. "Whatever happened here," she sighed, "it was quick."

She went on to say that some of the dead were wearing Army or military-type uniforms. Upon my further investigation, it was learned that a few of the 45 dead were recently discharged soldiers. They had survived the hell of war only to have their lives snuffed out, on their way home, in the sleepy town of Naperville.

And apparently they're still here.

Update:

In 2011, the paranormal research team of Beth Shields and Kirsten Tillman performed an EVP investigation at the railroad tracks, the very scene of the accident. Using the audio recorders, they asked out loud, "We asked before, but can we get some more names?" In response, a male voice was heard on the recording, responding, "Private Yeager."

When fellow investigator Chuck Kennedy pulled up a list of those killed in the train accident, one of the names listed was a military man by the name of Yeager.

HauntedNaperville.com

Naperville Ghosts

The Little Boy Who Sings Down the Lane...

People with questions and concerns regarding ghosts and paranormal subjects often contact me. Back in 2007 I received a phone call from a young lady who was concerned that she and her husband had a ghost in their Naperville home. She told me the following story...

She and her husband enjoy watching the ghost hunter-type programs on TV. They had recently watched a particularly exciting episode in which someone on the show spoke to the dead. As they sat on their couch talking about it, the husband commented that they should try it, too. The wife asked, "try what?" He said, "Talking to ghosts. The guys on TV do it and they're nothing special. I'll bet we could do it."

His wife agreed. It sounded like fun.

The next day she spent the afternoon online, looking for a process that would allow them to talk to the dead. Unfortunately, she found one. They decided to try it the following Saturday night.

She told me they had a great dinner and were eagerly anticipating their foray into ghostly conversation. It was about 9pm when they turned off all the lights in the house. They then sat opposite each other cross-legged on the living room floor, and set a white 10-inch pillar candle between them. He struck a match and lighted the wick. The room glowed in an eerie orange hue. The flickering flame caused shadows to dance on the walls around them. They were creeping out before they even started.

The procedure they were to follow instructed them to hold hands forming a circle around the burning candle. They did this. They were then to begin chanting over and over, with feeling, emphasis, and desire, "I want to talk to the dead. I want to talk to the dead. I want to talk to the dead. I want to talk to the dead. I want to ..."

According to the young lady, they were repeating the chant for about ten minutes when both of them noticed that the room had grown noticeably cooler. Neither mentioned it to the other; each thinking it was "just their imagination."

It wasn't.

After a few more moments of the chanting they heard a creaking door. They stopped chanting and both leaned over to look down their hallway – their bedroom door was closing - *by itself*. It was slowly shutting until it got about eight inches from being closed - at that point it slammed - *HARD*.

Their hearts skipped a beat as they looked at each other in shock. At that point the candle flame died out, leaving them in total darkness. The husband panicked. He jumped up, turned on the light, then grabbed the candle and threw it in the garbage can. They quickly embraced - their hearts racing. They agreed to never do anything like that again.

They got ready for bed, turned out the light, and got comfortable under the covers. They were having trouble getting to sleep – their hearts still racing as the events of the evening kept playing over and over in their heads. Just then, the silence of the night was broken by the sweet singing voice of a *young boy – in their room*!

The wife whispered, "Do you hear that?" The husband fumbled for the lamp switch and quickly turned on the light next to the bed. As soon as the light filled the room the room went silent. She asked, "Did you hear singing in this room?" The husband's face turned pale-white as he nodded a terrified '*yes*'.

The young lady told me that every once in a while they are awakened in their Naperville home by the sweet singing voice of a small ghost boy they inadvertently invited into their home by playing with the occult.

Naperville Ghosts

He Sits on Your Bed...

On Washington Street, a few miles south of downtown Naperville, a road intersects off to the east. It's called Royce Road. About a mile east on Royce Road a home sits unassumingly on a small hill.

In that home, a beautiful young lady named Kim and her 5-year-old son live with Kim's Mom. One night, in April of 2003, Kim and her Mom were up late watching the Tonight Show when their house suddenly shook with a violent crash. The two of them ran to their living room, the source of the noise, only to find that a pickup truck had crashed through the wall and was now parked in the house!

In the driver's seat, a young man, was covered in blood, and hunched over the steering wheel; he appeared to be dead. When the paramedics arrived they confirmed the fact that the young man was indeed dead.

Several days later, Kim's young son woke up from his nap crying hysterically. Kim ran in to comfort him. The boy, through his tears, told Kim that, "there is a scary man in my room." Being the wonderful mom that she is, Kim thoroughly checked her son's room; under the bed, in the closet, etc., She found nothing and assured her son that there was no one in the room. But, the boy insisted that the man had been there, saying, "He has lots of blood on him..."

A few nights later Kim was comfortable in her bed when was she gently awakened by the feeling of her mattress moving beneath her... Curiously, she wasn't concerned; Kim assumed it to be her son crawling on to the bed behind her, to "snuggle up to his mom." Kim turned to embrace her son - but, *he wasn't there.* Instead, the man *from the truck was sitting on the foot of her bed!* Kim told me, "I tried to scream and it wouldn't even come out." She said, "He just looked at me with these terrified eyes, and said, "I have no one to talk to..."

With that, the man faded away.

Kim and her Mom told me, that, on occasion, the man still appears in their home, doorknobs in the home sometimes rattle violently, and icy cold drafts move mysteriously through the house - *even to this day.*

Livingroom where truck entered house.

One of the doorknobs that violently shakes

Update:

A few years after the crash, a new neighbor moved in across the street from Kim and her mom. After the neighbor had been in the house for a couple months, she came over to Kim's house to introduce herself. When the small talk and pleasantries were over the woman asked Kim if she believed in ghosts. Kim, stunned, asked, "Why do you ask?"

The woman said, "I'm a Sensitive and I can often see spirits of the dead. The problem is that they look as real as humans do, so I don't always know what I'm actually seeing! But, a few weeks ago, as I was sitting on my porch, I saw a man in your back yard; he appeared to be just futzing around - I didn't think anything of it. That is until he went into your house by walking through the wall! I knew then that the guy was a spirit and not someone living here at the house."

Kim was blown away. She said, "Have I got a story for you..."

HauntedNaperville.com

The Streets of Naperville

The Whole Tooth

One of Naperville's unsung heroes of the Victorian era was Dr. A.B. Slick. Dr. Slick was one of the first Dentist's in Naperville.

His office was on the second floor of the building on the northeast corner where Jefferson Street meets Main Street. Curiously, the good doctor was also born in the building, as his parents owned it and ran a store on the street level. Being a dentist in Victorian times was of course much different than today. The cost to pull a tooth: 50 cents. To fill a tooth (the drill & fill): 1 dollar. And no one had dental insurance.

Because there wasn't electricity readily available when he started his practice, his first tooth drill was operated by *foot power*.

Have you ever noticed how few, otherwise beautiful, photographs taken during Victorian times actually depict a subject with a smile? People simply didn't smile in photos. Were they really that miserable? Actually yes, they probably were that miserable, but that's not the primary reason they weren't smiling. Generally they didn't smile because they had rotten teeth, or only a few teeth, or no teeth at all. It was a terrible situation.

Of course, false teeth were available to those who could afford them. But they were difficult to wear; painful, and they produced foul orders. In short, they weren't a practical solution. So what could a poor soul with rotten, or no, teeth do to fix his situation?

Strangely, this poor wretch could secure new teeth from a very unlikely source: a local *corpse*.

Here's how it worked. When someone died, still possessing relatively healthy teeth (generally a young person,) the undertaker would pull the teeth out. (Why bury perfectly good teeth?) He would immediately place the teeth into a cup of fresh milk to stall the decay process. The teeth would immediately be brought to a talented dentist, such a Dr. Slick.

The dentist knew which of his patients desired new chompers, so he'd quickly get one of them in the chair. He'd lean them back, open their mouth, and rip one of the offensive teeth out. Then, quickly, he'd grab one of the corpse teeth and *push it* into the hole just vacated by the rotten tooth! Believe it or not, the gums will literally "suck" the new tooth into the hole. The dentist would continue in this manner accordingly.

Generally speaking, the mouth never actually accepts the teeth as its own, and they'll probably only last about five years before they start to fall out, but, in the meantime, the patient has a new set of pearlies, *compliments of a local corpse.*

Naperville Ghosts

The Secret of Heatherton Hall

Secrets.

There are people today with horrific secrets. What goes on behind closed doors? There are secrets so disastrous, a person would do anything to keep them hidden away. Anything. Which of course would only lead to more secrets.

Is it possible that a secret is so horrific, so deplorable, that it must be kept hidden at any price? - A secret that can never be discovered, even if it must be protected from beyond the grave?

But, can a spirit actually do that?

Consider if you will, Janet's true story... Janet's aging mother had recently passed away. As Janet was going through her mother's home organizing for the estate sale, she'd hear a whisper in her ear "no...." She'd turn around; no one was there. "Strange," she thought, "it was so clear."

At times, while in the bedroom, she'd catch a strong whiff of her mother's perfume, and the air would chill. At other times, books would tumble off shelves. Knick-knack's would tip over on the dresser, sometimes crashing to the floor. But strangest of all, Janet would walk into the bedroom only to see things piled on her mother's bed that Janet had not put there...

Unnerved by it all, Janet secured the services of a psychic. The psychic went into the mother's bedroom alone and attempted to contact her. After a moment, the psychic emerged. She told Janet that her mother has been trying to convey a message to her – that there is money hidden in the bedroom mattress. The mother was concerned that the mattress was going to be tossed in the trash, cash and all.

The two women cut the mattress only to find that it was, indeed, the old woman's hiding place for her cash!

So spirits do have earthly fears and concerns. And, if properly motivated, they can manipulate physical materials. This is a very important fact.

The year was 1906. The place is a few acres of property on the south side of Naperville's Chicago Avenue; at the spot where Ellsworth Avenue currently intersects it, it is called Fort Hill. The grounds at the time are some of Naperville's most beautiful and lush, with a large spring-fed pond and rolling hills with high panoramic views of Naperville and the river to the south. Indeed, this was the perfect place for a wealthy businessman/lawyer named Judge John Goodwin to move his family.

Judge John Goodwin

The Judge was also a rancher. He had come from Kansas with a breed of cattle he had imported to America called Aberdeen Angus. Here, on this Naperville land, he introduced America to Angus beef.

The Fort Hill estate purchased by Judge Goodwin included the home of Louis Ellsworth. But for reasons never explained the Judge tore down the Ellsworth home and erected a massive southern style mansion. Could it be that the Ellsworth home had an unwelcome guest - in the form of Eva Ellsworth's ghost - that unnerved the good Judge? (See story included herein: The Flower of Fort Hill).

The new southern colonial home was a marvelous showpiece of DuPage County. The Judge named it Heatherton. Heatherton was straight out of "Gone With the Wind." It was everything you'd expect in a grand southern mansion home. It had a large porch complete with colonial style pillars complimenting the outside. When entering the spectacular home, you were greeted by a massive double stairway that met on the second floor balcony above the main hall foyer. No expense was spared. The home had lavish gardens, opulent furnishings, priceless artwork, oriental rugs, and perhaps one other thing, not quite so obvious – a secret.

For the next 10 years the Goodwin family rubbed elbows with the other Naperville elite. The Judge raised and sold his Angus cattle. He even served one term as City Attorney for the city of Naperville. Their home was always open to friends, neighbors, business associates and more. Glorious parties were thrown often. The Judge would host the yearly Kansas Society of Chicago. Their civic mindedness was legion; the Goodwin's were always the first to lend a hand or open their home in time of need. The good Judge referred to Naperville as "God's Country."

Then, in 1916, Judge Goodwin became seriously ill, often bedridden and weak. Diagnosed with a heart condition called angina pectoria, his health declined rapidly. Gone were the lavish parties. Gone were the spectacular outings on the grounds. Four servants wandered the grand edifice looking for tasks to keep them busy, so they might stay employed a little longer. Judge Goodwin and Heatherton laid quietly in the dark, slowly dying.

Several years passed, and on March 10, 1920, Judge Goodwin headed for downtown Chicago on urgent business. He took his family with him. They stayed at the Palmer House Hotel. Then, two days later, at 11:45p.m, on March 13, Judge John Goodwin died peacefully in his bed at the Palmer House Hotel, just a few days shy of his 62nd birthday.

Very strangely, just two hours after the Judge's death, his spectacular Heatherton Estate in Naperville burst into flames! The entire structure was reduced to ashes in a matter of hours! Subsequent investigations could not determine a cause for the blaze. Officially, it was ruled "Undetermined Cause." This means there is no reasonable explanation for why or how the fire started. So how did it happen? And is there significance to the timing?

Is it just an unbelievable coincidence that the Judge would die and then his estate randomly and mysteriously burst into flames two hours later? - And that the fire was so intense as to reduce, to a smoldering heap, this massive estate? All within three hours of his death 30 miles away?

Or, could there have been something inside the home the Judge did not want discovered? Could the Judge himself have come back, as did Janet's mother? Could he have ignited a flame the way Janet's mother knocked over books? Was he out to cover up a secret at all costs? Was his desperate plan, from beyond the grave, to reduce the home to rubble, destroying all evidence?

Were the incredible series of events that occurred on March 14, 1920 just an unbelievably horrific coincidence, or was there a secret of Heatherton Hall covered up by ghostly intervention?

Was there a secret in Heatherton Hall?

HauntedNaperville.com

HauntedNaperville.com

Naperville Ghosts

Happy Birthday to Me

Naperville's Catholic cemetery sits on land in the historic area of Naperville, at the intersection of North Avenue and Columbia Street. It was originally, in the 1840s, a cemetery for Germans who had settled in the area. Today it is the Saints Peter and Paul Catholic Cemetery. Today it is large, historic, beautiful, and... *haunted*.

One such haunt is one of the many Naperville haunts involving children.

Since May of 2009, there have been a handful of testimonies that report on a young girl, approximately 12 years old, is seen walking eastbound toward the cemetery down the sidewalk along North Avenue. She crosses Columbia Street, then, she walks through the cemetery fence and vanishes amongst the gravestones...

To see her walking along you would never assume her destination to be the cemetery, because, you see, she is dressed for a birthday party – complete with a helium party balloon.

Witnesses say the girl is Caucasian, with brown, shoulder length, hair. Her hair is very disheveled, tangled, and dirty looking. The girl is wearing a dark green dress that drags on the sidewalk around her. The dress is worn out and tattered. They say her left hand is holding tightly to a string – a string that anchors a single dark-colored helium-filled balloon.

Unlike other party-bound children, this paranormal party-goer, doesn't appear to be anticipating much laughter and fun; witnesses say she walks lazily along, staring toward the ground, with a look on her face of stern sadness.

One witness claimed that on the night of his encounter, as he walked along the street, he passed a fenced-in yard with a large dog in it. He says the dog didn't make a sound as he passed. But when the balloon-toting tot passed by the fence, the dog began barking loudly, even ferociously, at the small girl. Strangely, too, the girl didn't so much as flinch as the dog began its violent display - seemingly completely oblivious to it.

Perhaps strangest of all – the girl is *not alone*. She carries, on her back, in a small backpack of-sorts, what at first appears to be a doll – but as the girl draws closer it is clearly not a doll at all – but a small infant baby!

One witness claims the girl and her baby cargo passed him on the sidewalk, never acknowledging him. He watched the two youngsters as they passed by him, continuing east, crossing Columbia street, walking through the fence, and vanishing into the Sts. Peter & Paul Cemetery.

Strange place... –for a *party?*

The Streets of Naperville

Victorian Naperville and Premature Burial

For as long as humans have buried their dead, there has been a fear of premature burial. Few things are as terrifying as the thought that you could awaken from slumber to find yourself helpless in a pitch-dark wooden box buried in the earth.

The first President of the United States, George Washington, had a paralyzing fear of being prematurely buried, and he wasn't alone. Many people, especially the wealthy, provided detailed burial instructions that left no room for the unthinkable. Provisions such as: removing the heart, decapitation, or draining all the blood before burial.

The settlers of Naperville, in the Victorian Era, were comfortable with death itself, but the fear of pre-mature burial struck terror in most people. This fear was very real. Everyone knew that at anytime they could wake up buried alive! If they ate the wrong thing or became sick they could easily appear dead and be laid to rest. It could happen at any time to anyone.

If you think about premature burial, you'll notice that there is a problem with it. How did we discover that we were burying people who weren't dead? I mean, if we buried them six feet in the ground, how did we later discover the error? Were we digging up our dead?

Actually, *yes*.

You see all people are equal in the eyes of God on their deathbed. But the Victorian funeral wasn't about God or spirituality, and it was much more than simply a box, kind words, and a tombstone. The Victorian funeral was a show for your friends and neighbors. It was designed to symbolize, in your death, how important you were in life, and there were few things more disgraceful than a small funeral.

Many families would spend down to their last penny, and more, to make sure the outward expression of their loved one's funeral was a grand show of position and importance. This was done even at the cost of the family becoming a charity case from the expenditure. And this grand show is how a great many premature burials were discovered...

It wasn't unusual for a death to catch a family off guard. Without warning, they would have a corpse on their hands, a corpse that had to be laid to rest expediently. The undertaker was more than happy to oblige, but he required payment immediately. If the family was without money for the elaborate burial, they would have the undertaker discreetly lay the body to rest while the family began to sell everything they owned – clothes, furniture, livestock, jewelry, etc. – in an effort to raise the needed funds. Once the money was had, they paid the undertaker. He then would exhume the deceased and prepare a "more fitting and elaborate" send off.

Unfortunately, there were times when the undertaker would open the coffin only to discover that the deceased had pulled his hair out, or tried to claw his fingernails through the coffin lid! As these stories were relayed town to town, the fear of being the next victim became paralyzing.

In 1844, when Edgar Allen Poe released his classic novel "Premature Burial," the fear of pre-mature burial became full blown hysteria. In the novel, Poe describes the experience. "The unendurable oppression of the lungs, the stifling fumes of the damp earth, clinging to the death garments, the ridged embrace of the narrow house, the blackness of absolute night, the silence like a sea that overwhelms, and the unseen but palpable presence of the conqueror worm..."

The idea that at any time you could wake up in a buried coffin was something that caused quite a bit of anxiety in Naperville right up through the early 1900s. In fact, there is an article in the Naperville Clarion newspaper in 1915; the headline reads: "Absolute Proof of Death." The story goes on to say that there is no longer a need to fear pre-mature burial. A new injection has been developed that will identify the dead from those who appear to be dead. The developers of the injection insist that it is possible for a person to be very much alive, yet show no measurable signs of life. However, they assert, blood must move through anything that lives.

Therefore, blood is moving, however slowly, through the veins of those who *appear dead*.

The injection developed contains a harmless phosphorous dye. The dye is injected into the jugular vein – into the bloodstream. Within minutes, the moving blood of a living person will carry the dye to the pupils of the eyes and turn the white portion of the eyes green! If the eyes remain white, the dye has not been moved, and therefore, there is no circulation of blood, so the person is most certainly dead.

It appeared to be a worthwhile test; unfortunately, not everyone could afford to have it performed.

In 1911, an organization popped up called The Society for the Prevention of Premature Burial. They published a magazine called "The Perils of Premature Burial." In it they offered assistance in all aspects of death and burial, knowing that many people were without means for elaborate pre-burial tests.

They suggested that a bell be attached to a tombstone. To the bell was attached a string that was tied to one of the deceased's fingers. The deceased was then buried, attached string and all. Everyone was taught: "if you ever wake up underground, look for the string and start ringing!" But don't panic and pull too hard, because if the string breaks it will ruin your whole day! Ironically, the man who became very rich from the "string/bell" invention, was so obsessed with premature burial that he doused himself with oil and set himself on fire, committing suicide.

Often a cemetery worker or relative would stand watch in the graveyard overnight to listen for the bells. The often-used sayings such as "saved by the bell," and "graveyard shift," supposedly all came from this practice. Of course, not everyone could afford the special equipment needed for the bell alarm, so it was not unusual for a member of a poor family to sleep on top of the new grave for a few days, one ear in the dirt, listening for screams of terror.

Another suggestion was to include a shovel in the coffin with the deceased. I'm not sure a person could dig themselves out of those pitch-dark and tight quarters. But then again…

The situation was certainly different for the wealthy who had an easier go of it. One idea for them was to simply hire someone to sit with their corpse, watching and listening for signs of life. This was usually done in a mausoleum, sometimes for as long as 40 days!

The wealthy also had custom coffins equipped with a 4-inch wide tube that ran from the coffin lid all the way up to the cemetery surface. If any yelling was heard coming from the tube, the cemetery keeper could communicate through the tube that help was coming. As well, the unfortunate could breath through it until help arrived. On the other end of the spectrum, once the smell of bodily putrefaction was evident, the tube was removed.

There were also special nails developed that when driven into the coffin top to seal it, released a poison gas into the coffin, thereby guaranteeing a quick and painless death if unknowingly "the deceased" was still alive.

As embalming became more prevalent and mainstream, generally in the early to mid 1900s, the need for such measures were over, "'cause if you ain't dead when they start embalmin', you will be when they done."

The Streets of Naperville

Riding Off Into the Sunset

The Otto Kline story is an awe-inspiring epic, while at the same a gut-wrenching horror. He was the young Naperville boy with a dream, a dream he worked hard to make reality. And in so doing, he earned the respect of his peers, the love of his fans, and a dignified place in the annals of Naperville's illustrious history.

Otto Kreinbrink was a young Naperville boy growing up at the turn of the century, born in Naperville in 1887. Naperville at that time was at a crossroad as progress was beginning to creep into many facets of Naperville lives – including Otto's.

Otto's education was uneventful at the Naperville School. The school had about 300 students and 200 books. In an effort to keep order, the guidelines were simple: Try not to spit on the floor, bring a sponge to clean your slate; and do not use your knife to cut into your desk.

Young Otto grew up in a rustic Naperville. In the late 1800s an eel was caught in Mill Street Pond weighing 10-1/2 pounds! Also, rattlesnakes were not uncommon in and along the river.

Christmas in Naperville was growing in popularity during Otto's boyhood. Children wouldn't hang their stockings on the fireplace; they would hang them at the foot of their beds. The Hamilton Daniel's Drug Store (on Washington Street, west side, between VanBuren and Jefferson) was a favorite hangout of children, especially during Christmas time. Dr. Daniels had many Father Christmas decorations on display for children of all ages to enjoy. No doubt, Otto's parents would have frequented this Naperville gem.

Naperville looked quite a bit different, too. In the 1800s the streets were two feet lower than the sidewalks to allow for an easier entrance and exit from a horse drawn carriage. There were hitching posts along the streets and gas powered light poles. Water Street, now Chicago Avenue, was the center of town. The telephone was available in Naperville in the mid 1880s. Naperville's first telephone line was a 2-phone system that ran from the Beckman Harness Shop on Washington Street and Jackson up to the Beckman home on the corner of Chicago and Loomis.

In 1895, an incredible new form of entertainment called the "moving picture theater" was set up in a tent on Washington near Jefferson during the summer months. Otto may have been inspired to the grand scale of his passion after watching a rugged cowboy short film on a hot summer night. Of course, there was also the local inspiration of Beckman's Harness Shop and Naperville horse shows on Aurora Avenue to fuel his fire.

By 1900, Naperville's population had grown to 2,600, and this boy Otto, was determined to be a standout. He poured himself into his love of horses and riding. Every available moment he spent focused on becoming the greatest trick rider ever. He was going to be somebody, somebody important, no matter how hard he had to work.

And work he did.

There was a horse pen at the west end of Spring Avenue, and everyday after school Otto would sneak in and ride one of the horses. He most often had to ride bareback. On Chicago Avenue, near the Naperville Country Club, there was another stable, and Otto used to practice his horse riding tricks there.

He was about 16 when he took the stage name "Kline," his mother's maiden name. He then kissed his mom on the forehead and headed to Montana to find fame, fortune, and his dream. There, anyone who would give him a chance to show his stuff was glad they did. This kid was special. He was goin' places, that was clear.

As the years went by, Otto proved himself to be one-of-a-kind. He went on to win medals at Pendleton, Oregon and Denver. He performed in such shows as Arizona Joe, Buffalo Bill, Annie Oakley, Sitting Bull, and others. He was living his dream. Naperville couldn't be more proud.

> —Otto Krienbrink is spending several days with relatives here. He has been scoring great success with his rope throwing stunts in the large vaudeville houses of the country the past year.

This snippet from the Naperville newspaper, dated January 1912, says Otto was visiting with family in Naperville at that time.

At 26, he began performing with Barnum & Bailey. At 27, he received first honors in the Famous Stampede Day in Winnipeg, Canada, as well as Cheyenne's Frontier Day contest. At 28, he married a beautiful aerialist performer and was the featured performer at New York's Madison Square Garden. Not bad for a Naperville boy with a dream.

It was Tuesday, April 20, 1915. Madison Square Garden, afternoon show. Over 5,000 fans had come to experience the finest riders and performers in the world.

That morning, Otto had received a telegram from his wife of one month. It explained that her show in Baltimore had been cancelled, so she was coming to New York on Saturday to be with him. Otto was beside himself excited.

The Tuesday show had gone exceptionally well. Otto, being the featured performer, closed the festivities. He performed many of the stunts and shenanigans that his fans had come to expect and be thrilled by. He was finishing up with a genuine crowd pleaser; he called it the Vault Trick. Basically, the horse runs past him at full gallop, Otto vaults up and mounts the horse without touching the reins - as the horse flies past him! Unbelievable.

Otto stood at one end of the arena, and Kitty, his favorite horse, at the other end. He whistled to her and she began running toward him. Her nostrils flared. Her hooves threw up dirt from the ground, as the thunderous pounding grew more intense. Otto bent his knees slightly, turning toward her. He smiled as she closed in on him. He looked into her eyes as her head went past him and he leapt into the air.

In that split second, Otto Kline lay on the ground, unconscious. His head split open gushing blood in the dirt. Something had gone terribly wrong. Otto missed his mark, falling behind Kitty, as her right hind hoof struck him squarely in the forehead. Before anyone could react, Kitty stopped on a dime and walked back to Otto. She knew she'd hurt him.

Otto was taken to Bellevue hospital, never regaining consciousness. He died three hours after the accident.

How could he have made such an error? Riding was second nature to him. Some of his friends felt that his wife's letter was responsible for his accident, in that he may have been preoccupied in anticipation of her arrival. Others feel that a cut on his hand from a loose tack on a saddle horn may have weakened his hand or caused the loss of concentration. The wound was serious enough for Otto to mention it in a letter to his wife just two days before his death. Those who saw the wound described it as an ugly gash on the same hand he used for the Vaulting Trick. We'll never know.

His wife accompanied Otto's remains to Naperville Cemetery, where he was laid to rest. A tombstone fit for a humble cowboy giant marks his gravesite. His fellow performers commissioned the cowboy tombstone – a stone that will forever mark the burial place of a true Naperville son.

At one time, his photographic image was on the stone, but a few too many tear-stained touches have taken their toll. For many years, a chamber was next to the headstone so that his fans could leave messages to him as well as flowers.

Otto's reputation won him awards and friends all over the country, but he was always a Naperville boy inside.

Adios Buckaroo.

HauntedNaperville.com

Naperville Ghosts

Fright Night

The building is often overlooked when observing the unique 19th century architecture in downtown Naperville. It is somewhat plain to the eye. But the building at 103 West Jefferson, northwest corner of Jefferson & Main, has a colorful history and leaves a trail of unexplained paranormal encounters in its wake.

Haunted Fright Night building, 2007

This building is about 150 years old, and although today it is simply two-story retail space, it at one time was quite a downtown hotspot. Originally the building was larger, extending north down Main Street.

In the late 1800s this was Nadelhofer's general store. Back then, there was a wooden sidewalk wrapping around the place – a sidewalk most likely installed by the women of Naperville! The ladies grew tired of trudging through mud and muck, so they laid Naperville's first sidewalks themselves, using scraps leftover from the construction of Plank Road!

In around 1900, Arthur and Gladys Hesterman purchased the building. They added a bowling alley in the portion of the building that extended north on Main. It burned down shortly thereafter leaving the building at its present size.

Originally the upper floor was a Victorian apartment while the ground floor was retail space. Arthur and Gladys Hesterman, lived upstairs and operated a tavern below. When Mr. Hesterman died in the early 1900s, Mrs. Hesterman continued living upstairs but closed her tavern and began renting the retail space to another tavern proprietor. It became Clark's Tavern.

Naperville has never had a shortage of taverns; they lined the streets. In fact, across Jefferson Street from Clark's Tavern was the Red Top Tavern, on the southwest corner of Jefferson & Main. It was an upscale drinking establishment with a large outdoor patio seating area on Main Street. Being upscale, women were allowed inside, but not without conditions. One condition being the entrance, photos of the Red Top Tavern show a doorway on Jefferson Street clearly marked "Ladies Entrance."

Records are unclear but it appears that Gladys died in the 1930s, at which point the building changed owners and Kenny Clark's hamburgers operated on the spot. After that, Jimmy Fiddler's Hamburgers opened in the building. Fiddler's was a red hot Naperville hangout for decades.

In 2007, this author rented the second floor of the building to use as offices for the operation of the Naperville Ghost Tour business. The upstairs, having been an apartment originally, was divided up into several rooms. At the top of the entrance stairs was a small foyer, with a few rooms branching out from there.

To the left was a room that would have served as a bedroom. Next to that room was a bathroom, and continuing to the right was a kitchen.

Large windows in both the living room and dining room provide not only lots of natural light for the upstairs but beautiful views of Jefferson and Main Streets.

Many "curious" events unfolded within the walls of 103 West Jefferson, the spirits often making themselves clearly present.

When we took rental possession of the upstairs, we were made aware of a ghostly tale connected to the property. At first, I was suspicious of its authenticity because I couldn't substantiate it. Then, one day, a lady came to the property to buy tickets for the tour. She walked in and asked me if I was aware that the building was haunted. I replied that I'd heard a story but that was all. She asked if the story I heard involved a small boy who talked with a ghost. I responded, "Yes." She said the story is true because she knows the lady it happened to! I asked her to share her story with me so I could compare the two versions. The stories were exactly the same!

So here for you now - for the first time in print - is the true ghost story of 103 West Jefferson Avenue.

I'm Talking to the Old Lady

Several decades ago, a young lady rented the upstairs of the building for her new business. She and a few friends spent an entire day moving her in. They brought store fixtures, furniture and inventory into the upstairs retail place. She arranged and rearranged it all until it was perfect. She went home exhausted.

The next day was her first day in business. Very excited, she inserted her key in the lock. She turned it. She heard the deadbolt disengage. She pushed the door open and peered inside. She stopped. There was uneasiness thick in the air. She felt the presence of something. "Anybody in there?" she asked. No answer. She started up the stairs. They creaked under her foot, seemingly louder than before.

As she got to the top of the stairs, she cautiously peered into the store. She couldn't believe what she saw. The furniture had been moved around. It was clear to her that nothing substantial had been taken; things were just rearranged. She quickly called the landlord. "Someone has a key to my store," she screamed. "They were in here last night!"

There was quiet on the other end of the phone.

After a moment, the landlord sighed, saying, "There was someone in there last night, but no one has a key..." He went on to explain that every once in a while, a playful spirit who resides in the building likes to make itself known. It appears to be harmless, if not a little - bold.

"That's absurd," the woman said. "Someone has a key, and I'm holding you responsible when things go missing." She slammed the phone down.

Things were uneventful for a few days, that is, until that Saturday. The woman brought her 6-year-old son to the shop because he was off school. There were no customers in the store and the woman was finishing up some bookwork in the back room, her son was out in the store. Suddenly, she heard her son giggle. She smiled to herself. Then she heard him say out loud, "No!" There must be a customer out there, she thought. She quickly proceeded to the store area, and as she rounded the corner, she saw her son sitting on the floor engaged in a conversation with someone who wasn't there. She looked around the room - no customer in the store. She observed her son. He laughed and talked and waited for a response as if actually communicating with someone.

She interrupted him, "Who are you talking to?"

He responded, "The old lady, mom."

"What lady?"

"Forget it..."

Every once in a while, the lady would talk to the boy again. The woman never spoke to the lady, but the furniture would, on occasion, find its way to other parts of the room....

The Haunted Dining Room where small boy would speak to old woman.

Is the spirit still active? Take the following examples, all from the fall and winter of 2007...

A Whistle from Another Time

One of the Fright Night owners, Lisa, was working late one night painting in the store. The night was very quiet, nothing but the hum of the air conditioners and an occasional telephone ring.

That's when she heard it... a very faint whistling. Like a person whistling a song. Lisa quickly went outside to see if it was coming from the street. Nope. She came back in. She stood on the spot where she was before, and there it was! She listened for a few minutes, and then said out loud, "Whoever you are, we know you are here, and we hope you approve of the work we are doing." With that, the whistle faded away!

A few days later, Kevin was there early to meet with a utility worker. He was standing in the dining room. Things were very quiet, and that's when the whistling started! Kevin listened intently to it. It sounded like someone sitting on a porch swing whistling a church hymn. It only lasted a moment or two and then faded away.

That Was Weird...

Kevin was seeing a client about a video production project. They were standing at the counter in the store. It was mid-afternoon, and they were alone. Kevin was relaying the ghost stories about the building when the woman commented, "I don't much believe in ghostly stuff." Kevin nodded. Then a loud thud could be heard behind the woman. It startled both of them. They looked on the floor behind the woman, There on the ground lay a large purse that had been on the shelf! Just as the woman said that she didn't believe in ghosts, the purse tumbled off the shelf to the floor!

The woman looked at Kevin confessing, "That was weird..." Kevin replied, "Yes, it was..."

The Crosses Crashed

One day, we had received a shipment of decorative crosses, of various sizes. Most of them were displayed on the window ledges in the dining room, very sturdy places. That night, the four people working the store left at about 9:30 p.m. When Kevin came in the next morning, two of the crosses had been smashed on the floor of the dining room! They did not appear to have fallen down. They were smashed on the floor, as if thrown, *hard*.

There were 12 crosses on display, only two were smashed! And they weren't from the same shelf! All the others were fine.

Creepy Creak

Whenever anyone entered the stairway of the building and began their assent to the second floor, the staircase would creak loudly under their weight. It was an easy way to know that someone had entered the building. It wasn't foolproof though - because there were many cases in which loud creaking noises were distinctly heard coming from the stairway and there was no one visible on the stairs!

Are You There, Gladys?

In December of 2007, a séance was held in the dining room of the building. The objective was to contact the spirit, or spirits, of the building. The psychic who was brought in wasn't told about the building's history or ghostly past.

It was about 10 p.m. when several people, including the psychic, sat comfortably around an antique dining room table in the center of the dining room. The room was illuminated only with taper candles on the table and in wall sconces. The psychic commented that the spirit energy in the room was very active - before the séance had even begun...

A paranormal investigator named Alex Felix was handling the technology side of the séance. He was recording it with audio tape, taking photos, and using EMF meters (devices that measure spikes in electromagnetic energy, a common indicator of spirit presence). This author was there as an observer.

The psychic quieted the room and asked those seated to join hands. She closed her eyes and began asking the spirits to communicate with her. Only a few moments had passed when she turned to me and said, "I'm hearing the name Gladys. Is that significant?" Honestly, I almost fell over.

I said, "As far as we know, the spirit here is named Gladys." The psychic nodded and said, "She's here right now."

I asked, "Is she happy we're here?" The psychic asked Gladys the question. After a moment she looked at me and said, "Gladys is only unhappy with what you have done with her bedroom in the back. She says it's too messy. She spends a lot of time there and feels uncomfortable in there.

I told Alex to quickly go to Gladys' room and see if he can get a photo of her spirit.

He was soon in the room. The psychic said that Gladys was in there with him. Alex began taking digital photos. Nothing unusual showed up on them. The psychic said in an elevated voice, "Gladys, if you're in there you have to make yourself known. Alex is in there too." With that, the EMF meter Alex held began slowly beeping, indicating a spike in electromagnetic energy around him.

The psychic sighed, "Thank you, Gladys."

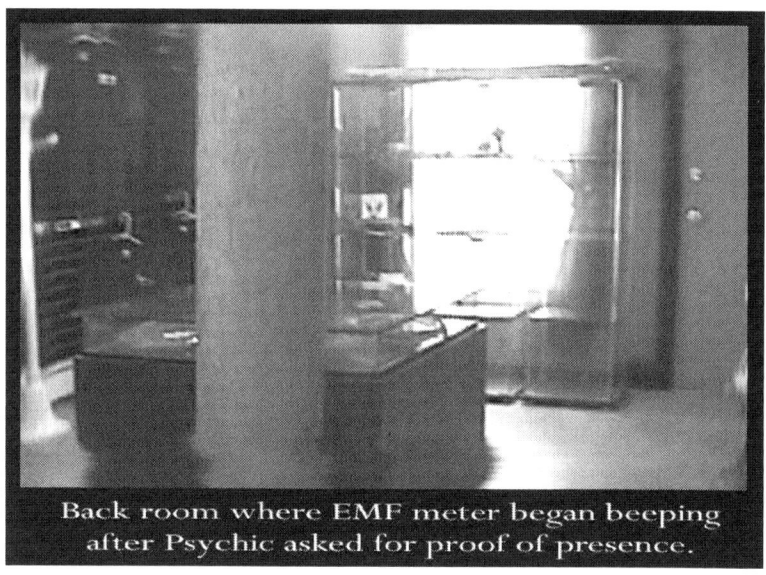
Back room where EMF meter began beeping after Psychic asked for proof of presence.

As mentioned before, the earliest occupation of the building we can find is that of the Nadelhofer General Store. Curiously, Nadelhofer's was one of the first undertaker families in Naperville. Did they run a portion of the undertaking business from this location? Is that related to the haunt?

In the early 1900s, Mrs. Hesterman owned the property, living upstairs and renting out the ground floor. Could she be attached to the property?

The little boy mentioned earlier did say he was talking to an "old lady."

186

HauntedNaperville.com

The Streets of Naperville

Naperville's Wicked Witch

We are all familiar with the Salem Witch Trials, but few realize that the terror continued through the 1800s and early 1900s. Many people, mostly women, were dragged into American courts on the charge of being a witch! Evidence was presented; witnesses testified; and jury's decided fates on such testimony as: "I saw horns sprout from her head!" "She killed my dog, just by looking at him!" And other such testimony was actually admitted. Thankfully, jury's saw through the lunacy and all defendants were acquitted.

But, what did emerge from that display was the prevailing belief that people can be very much concerned about their neighbors who may be a little bit... *different*. And Naperville was absolutely no exception. Case in point: this is the true story of Naperville's Wicked Witch.

Currently, on the northeast corner of Main Street and Van Buren Street, is a parking garage. But back in the early 1900s - way before Naperville had parking garages - this corner was part of the residential area and the location of a tattered old frame house. And in that house lived a very old woman.

Her eyes were dark and lifeless. Her face was stark and sunken with deep creases in hanging skin that swung when she moved. She was haggard? Sure. Was she nasty? Oh yeah. Was she mean? You bet. Was she alone? Always. Was she a... *witch*?

There are some who remember her as "Old Terese." They claim she would walk Naperville's downtown sidewalks with a purposeful stride, though it appeared she never had anywhere to go. She'd be wearing the same old tattered cloak and cap everyday. When she'd pass a woman wearing hoops she'd rant and rage at them, scaring them silly. Many would cross the street if they saw her coming their way.

It's not however that her neighbors didn't try to befriend her, not through the difficult façade. She did receive invitations for afternoon teas and such from the other women in town. Most often she declined, but when she did accept she made things quite difficult for her host; they say that when she entered her host's house she had her own little "ritual" as she stepped in:

She would look to the floor, and if she spotted a rug she would roll it up or at the least peer under it. Some feel that this custom comes from the fear that the invitation was a lure into the house and the rug on the floor is there to cover a large hole that is a trap for her to fall into - when she stepped on the rug, down she would go into the pit! She was just making sure that the floor was solid under the small rugs.

Once assured that the floors were safe, she would make her way around the room "disabling" the mirrors by either covering them or turning them toward the wall! Was there something about her reflection that caused her dis-ease? Or, could it be as others suggest: since mirrors can be portals, used by ghosts and demons, to move about from dimension to dimension, she wanted to eliminate that "traffic" in the room? Either way, her behavior upon entering a home was certainly cause for suspicion that there unique things going on with this old woman!

Sometimes when you were on your way to school, market, or park, you'd have to use the sidewalk in front of her house, and, if you looked at her window you might see her ugly weathered wrinkled face peering out from behind a filthy and stained curtain! She was holding the curtain off to the side with a shaking hand. Her dark, glazed-over, eyes watched you very closely - why?

Anyone who had an interaction with her came away feeling a little uneasy. The prevailing opinion around town was, "Don't get on her bad side, or you may end up living your life as a frog!" All the kids knew better than to mess with her, and the adults generally stayed out of her way.

One day there was a lot of commotion in downtown Naperville. It seems that there were a lot of people experiencing what could only be described as "ghosts" on their property! The experiences varied but the gist of the complaints were: They heard rustlings in their fields and yards, but when they investigated the ruckus, there was nothing there. They'd hear pounding on their roofs, and when they'd investigate, there was nothing there. Pets and farm animals would be torn apart and devoured on the grounds, but no one heard or saw anything! Trash would get strewn about, but there was no obvious cause.

Most of the peculiar activity was taking place in the area of Naperville that was bounded by Ogden Avenue on the north, Washington Street on the east, Jefferson Street on the south, and River Road on the west. This unsettling activity went on all summer.

The people of Naperville were very freaked out.

One day a few women were standing on the corner of Van Buren & Main talking about the strange goings-on in the town, they were very concerned. They were sharing their fears with each other and trying to comfort one another when they heard what sounded like a sinister laugh... They looked around for the source, and that's when they saw - it was the witchy woman. From where she was she had overheard the women talking and found their fear very amusing.

"What is so funny"? One woman asked. The witch stared off in the distance, raised her arm, and pointed her crooked finger to the east, demanding, "Go back to your rats den all of you!" The woman were terrified of her and scurried off as the witch was heard snickering to herself once more.

Then, a few weeks later, in the early autumn, a man was driving down Ogden Avenue, eastbound. He was just a little west of Mill Street, when he saw something run out in front of his car. He slammed on the brakes to avoid hit it, but he hit it anyway. He thought it might have been a large dog or coyote. He quickly leapt from his car and looked underneath only to discover a bobcat under his wheels! It was dead. As he news spread through town, no one could believe it. A black bobcat? - In this area? The whole town was talking about it.

After a couple days the bobcat was old news and the people went back to talking about their ghost. And that's when they realized that the ghostly, unexplained noises in the area had stopped, no one had a new encounter to talk about. The townspeople concluded that the bobcat must have been the culprit all along, and there was no ghost. The bobcat was on the roofs, killing the livestock, and all. He must have been impossible to see in the dark. Mystery solved.

All was well.

Well, *almost.*

You see, at the same time that the bobcat mystery got solved, another mystery popped up: where did the witchy woman go? She was no longer in her house. She had vanished into thin air! She was just... gone. To this day no one knows what happened to her.

But there are those old timers who had run-ins with the old hag who insist that if the bones of that bobcat could be found, we might discover that they are actually the bones of a frail... old... witch.

Authors note: This story was told to the author by an old-timer in a Naperville restaurant, he claims it is true. I have tried to find substantiation for it and have only found pieces. Such as: a woman acknowledged an old woman named Terese who used to turn pictures and mirrors to the wall. Another remembers "the witch on VanBuren." A young man I spoke to remembers the bobcat being struck. The investigation continues.

It may seem strange to us that the townspeople thought that they had done something to bring a ghost upon them, but the early 1900s found the streets of Naperville ringing with many strange tales...

<u>Actual stories being talked about:</u>

* A story from Romania in which unbaptized ghost babies are heard crying out for their mothers. Unfortunately, the ghosts can't be appeased until their graves are sprinkled with holy water every day for seven years!

* A story from Africa of a ghost dog. A family dog was struck and killed by a train. After that, the train whistle began blowing more frequently. Upon complaining of the noise the family learned that the engineer was just trying to scare a dog that was often on the track. The description of the dog was the same as the dog that had been killed.

* The warning that new brides and grooms must be protected from witches. In order to ward off the witch's evil, several precautions must be taken: Only use gray horses to pull any carriages, none of the wedding guests can wear black or green, the engagement ring can't contain opals or emeralds, and the wedding can't be performed in any month containing an "A" in its name!

Given these topics that concerned them, it's easy to see how the town could get caught-up in the belief that their problems had supernatural roots.

The Streets of Naperville

Burying Naperville's Dead

From a pioneer newspaper:

"The common belief is that the Undertaker is the happiest of all tradesmen. After all, he boldly charges for the best coffin, mattress and pillow, yet, in years to come, who will doubt the quality?"

HauntedNaperville.com

The Naperville Cemetery - Est. 1850

Naperville's Undertakers

In 1831, Joe Naper settled the town that was to bear his name. And ever since then, the business of burying Naperville's dead has been a healthy one. Despite Naperville's age, only a handful of undertakers have seriously practiced undertaking on our streets.

Undertakers in pioneer times were generally a town's carpenters as well. Evidently, the craft of building a coffin from wood required a skilled hand.

It appears that Naperville's first "official" undertaker was Philip Orcutt. Some of those who followed in his footsteps were: William Nadelhofer, Fred Long, the Beidelman brothers, John Kraushar, Friedrich, Jones, and Kunsch.

Philip Orcutt was in the undertaking business in Naperville as early as 1855; Naperville was just 24 years old. His solicitations claimed he "would attend to all business performed by an undertaker." This, according to his advertisements, included: made-to-order burial cases and caskets, as well as a horse-drawn Hearse.

William Nadelhofer and Ed Stutenrath were in the carpentry and coffin business in Naperville as early as June of 1857. In addition to coffins, they produced bureaus, tables, chairs, mattresses, sofas and stands. They were located on Jefferson Street, south side, about the center of the street (two doors west of the Naperville Bank).

It's unclear if these two carpenters were in the business of *actually burying* the dead in 1857. But, by August of 1861, The DuPage Press had an ad for the company that reported, "a Hearse is now available." Also at this time, Ed Stutenrath was no longer a part of the business, and William Nadelhofer independently took on the roll of "Undertaker to the Naperville Cemetery." Nadelhofer begins advertising "coffins of all sizes, and made to order."

In the 1850s, there was a cabinetmaker on Washington Street named John Bentz. It isn't clear if Bentz was in the burial business, but being a carpenter meant he in all likelihood built the coffins. In about 1859 a man from LeLand, Illinois, named Fred Long, began training with John Bentz, learning the cabinet-making business.

Fred Long - Undertaker

In about 1861 Fred Long opened a carpentry and undertaking business in Naperville. It was located at 231 S Washington. Whether Long also learned the undertaking business from Bentz is not known.

Fred Long's business as it sat on Washington Street.

It was through Fred Long that Naperville's most successful undertaking establishment came to be. Fred Long was the uncle to two young men named Arthur and Oliver Beidelman. The young men lived with their aunt and uncle in Naperville and learned the undertaking craft from him. Arthur was only 17 in 1894 when he had the responsibility of tending to horses used in the family business, as well as the duty of retrieving the dead from Naperville homes.

In 1906, Arthur felt the itch to go out on his own. He set up a monument carving (tombstone) business at 318 S Washington. Then, in 1909, an undertaking and funeral business was being run by the Beidelman's at 35 S. Washington.

In 1911, Fred Long was retiring and sold his business to his nephew, Oliver Beidelman. Actually, it wasn't sold; it was traded! Oliver traded the home he and his wife owned on Chicago Avenue for Fred Long's funeral business. They then moved into an apartment above the monument business at 318 S Washington.

The Beidelman furniture, monument, undertaking, and ambulance businesses flourished in Naperville. In about 1926, the Beidelman's realized the need for more space for their business. They had admired a building in Wheaton for its size and design. It was a three-story brick building in the Prairie Gothic style. They decided to build a copy of it in Naperville.

In 1928 at a cost of $2,000, the building that sits currently on the northwest corner of Washington and Jackson was constructed. Oddly, the Wheaton structure that inspired it has long since been demolished.

When it was constructed, it did not have the portion of the building to the north, where Penzie's Spices currently is. There was a small home on that land. Later the Beidelman family removed the home and added the large brick addition, using it as a funeral chapel. If you look closely at the upper front of the building, you can see where the spectacular Prairie Gothic chapel windows once were.

The Beidelman Funeral Parlor now a retail store...

While the Beidelman's were building their business, another undertaker/furniture maker set up shop in Naperville. The year was 1907 when John Kraushar, a talented German craftsman, opened his business at 10 E. Jefferson.

The John Kraushar Building on Jefferson Street, just east of Washington. The phone number was 322.
(Still standing)

The John Kraushar funeral business in Naperville was one of the most up-to-date funeral establishments in the nation in 1912. According to the newspaper, in 1912, "John Kraushar has added a gray ambulance casket wagon. This making him one of the most up-to-date outfits in the country."

Mr. Kraushar's furniture business may also be responsible from bringing recorded music to Naperville. His appears to be the first business in Naperville selling the Victor Victrola Talking Machine.

In about 1919, an undertaker named Chris Friedrich opened for business at 16 E. Jefferson. By 1920, Chris Friedrich and John Kraushar were business partners. Friedrich also had a furniture store. By 1928, Friedrich was an independent undertaker once more. Also, he had moved to 20 E. Jefferson and added ambulance service to his business.

Coffins, and Preparing the Dead

The assassination of President Lincoln in 1856 changed funerals forever. For the first time, the decomposition of a human body had to be halted or curtailed. The long funeral train ride from Washington D.C. to Illinois would test the limits of a new science known as Mortuary Science.

Through the 1800s, the funerals in Naperville were hurried affairs. Because of decomposition, a person was most often buried within two days of their death. Most were buried in a simple pine box after a short funeral service in their home or local church. Following the service, the coffin was loaded on a horse-drawn wagon for its "final journey" to the cemetery.

The journey was a dramatic affair. Often the only sounds heard were the squeaking of the wheels, the creaking of the wagon, the clip-clop of the horse hooves on the street, and the lonesome clang of the church bell that rang out in dirge-like fashion.

In July of 1870, Fred Long began offering the services of a horse-drawn "hearse." This elaborate method of transporting a coffin was in keeping with Victorian style, and was available in Naperville in 1870.

Horse-drawn Hearse 1870

Undertakers of the time wore only black. Most people would consider this an effort on the part of the undertaker to share the mourning of those around him, but this isn't the case. Undertakers believed that the wearing of black would keep malevolent spirits away from them.

As the 1900s moved in, the "wake" was added to the burial ritual. Many feel the wake came about during the premature burial scare of the late 1800s. The wake was a few days to observe the deceased and make sure he wasn't going to "wake" up! Because of the delay in burial, the deceased needed to be prepared for burial, much the same as President Lincoln had 50 years before. And thus, embalming began growing in popularity.

Coffins too, became more elaborate and were built with more resilient materials than wood. In 1911, Beidelman's began offering "The Egyptian" coffin, a product that was guaranteed to be both air and watertight!

By 1916, Beidelman's was offering burial vaults constructed of concrete, as well as steel units.

Transporting the coffin also got high-tech with the invention of the "Horseless Hearse." Beidelman funeral services in Naperville had available two types of Hearse – horse-drawn or automotive.

Beidelman Autohearse used in Naperville

The process of embalming, though primitive, was available in Naperville in the early 1900s. In the beginning it was simply the process of draining the blood. This was usually done in the kitchen of the deceased's home!

Kitchens of the time were ideal for the process for several reasons: the kitchen was out of the way; it generally had running water and a sink; and most importantly, kitchens had hard floors, which made it easier to clean up messes....

As we progressed into the 1920s, embalming became more sophisticated. It was usually started with an incision in a main artery where the embalming fluid is pumped in. Meanwhile, at another area of the body, an incision is made and blood is removed at the same time, thereby filling the veins and arteries with a preservation agent, often formaldehyde. A vacuum is inserted in various "bodily orifices" and removes the contents of the intestines and the stomach. They are then also filled with embalming fluid. Makeup and cotton are used to add color and to "lift" areas of the face and hands that are sunken.

Beidelman funeral services, in the early 1920s, charged $5 for an adult embalming. The funeral chapel on Washington Street was free to use.

Beidelman Ad - 1926

The individual with the responsibility of burials in the cemetery, as well as the general maintenance of a graveyard, was the Sexton.

In the 1920s, the Sexton for the Naperville Cemetery published the fees for the various services they offered:

A "rough box" burial was available in Naperville Cemetery into the 1920s, the sexton charged between $9 and $10 depending on the size of the coffin.

The additional fee for a cement or steel vault was $10.

If you required additional "lining and trimming," there was an extra fee of $3.

The graves of children were charged at $1.25 per linear foot.

The charge for mowing and caring for a cemetery lot was $5 per year. Perpetual Care Insurance was also available, providing care and maintenance of the gravesite indefinitely. Its cost was between $50 and $175 - based on the size of the grave plot.

HauntedNaperville.com

Tombstones and Flowers

It's been said, "We don't erect a tombstone because someone died - we erect a tombstone because someone lived."

It's a nice sentiment. But the truth is, it goes a lot deeper than that. In old Europe and Romania, the living were dreadfully afraid of the dead because they believed that the dead can come back to terrorize and kill. They can come back as zombies, or vampires, or witches, or monsters, or...

Sheer terror would erupt with every burial.

Necessity being the mother of invention, someone along the way thought of putting a huge rock on top of the fresh grave to hinder the corpse in its efforts to leave the earth. "That'll keep grandpa down..." they thought. They were right; people slept better.

Along the way someone thought to put the name of the deceased on the rock, and today we have the headstone.

There is no doubt that headstones are beautiful. Some are even works of art and sculpture. They are a physical acknowledgement of a life lived. They are often therapeutic, giving the bereaved a place to mourn and, as such, assisting greatly in the healing process.

But none of this was the original intent - the terrifying need to quell the paralyzing fear that our dead loved-ones would reanimate in the ground; that their hands and arms would slowly rise from the cold soil and they would supernaturally extricate themselves from the damp earth that encased them. There they would seek out the living to satisfy an unfathomable and diabolical need. And we, the victims, would be attacked in the night...

Just one casual look in any of the Naperville cemeteries and it becomes very clear that Napervillians have always taken tombstones very seriously. Our cemeteries have some of the most large and elaborate monuments to be found anywhere. And the monument cutter has been a Naperville institution since our town's beginning.

As early as 1850, Naperville had a gravestone cutter. The company was A.S. Sherman & Company. They may well be the first in a line of successful tombstone businesses in Naperville...

Also in the 1850s was Kailer Monument Company. They were located on the northeast corner of Washington and Benton Streets. Many of our town's early tombstones were produced there.

In 1906, Arthur Beidelman opened a monument business at 318 S. Washington. Not limited to tombstones, they also produced burial vaults, markers, vases, and birdbaths. It was here that Beidelman introduced Naperville to the electronic process of cutting and sanding both granite and marble.

In 1907, a German named Wunderlich opened a company called "Naperville Monument Works," which offered all types of tombstone and monument production. It was located on Jefferson Street, one door east of the City Hall.

The earliest funeral florist in Naperville was a man named Charles Rohr. He was in business in 1907.

Florist, Charles Rohr

Naperville's Cemeteries

At first glance it would appear that Naperville's dead are buried in one of two graveyards: Naperville Cemetery or Saints Peter and Paul Cemetery. And this is *mostly true.*

In our town's humble beginnings, way before Naperville Cemetery and Saints Peter & Paul Cemetery, our dead ended up in places that we would never suspect today...

In the spring of 1832, the Black Hawk War erupted. Joe Naper and other townsmen built a large fort on the top of a high hill on Chicago Avenue just east of Washington Street. They called the fort "Fort Payne." And the hill came to be known as "Fort Hill."

To this day, the top of the hill where the south side of Ellsworth Street intersects Chicago Avenue is called Fort Hill. Because of its natural beauty and panoramic views of the river and city, all through the 20th Century the hill had been utilized recreationally year round. Whether it was tobogganing in the winter, picnics in the summer, a student's out-of-the-way study place, or just a quiet springtime nap under a favorite tree, the hill has been a popular place for Napervillians to gather.

But few people who have spent time on the hill know that the hill they are enjoying was also Naperville's first burial ground!

Those killed in the Black Hawk War were buried along side Fort Payne. In addition, when the Black Hawk War was over and the fort dismantled, pioneer and Indian dead continued to be buried on the hill.

Naperville's hidden cemetery - on Fort Hill

There were several other cemeteries in use in the area through the mid 1800s. The Erb family, who owned a farm on the northeast corner of Mill and Bauer Streets, donated a small corner of their land to be used as a public burial ground, known as Erb Cemetery. Today it is overgrown with thick brush and trees, but this corner lot at the northwest corner of Mill and Bauer Streets, near the Cress Creek subdivision, was used as a public burial ground.

Hidden Erb Cemetery on NW Corner of Mill & Bauer Streets

There were also two other cemeteries in use early on, even before Joe Naper settled the town. They are the Vermont Cemetery, and Big Woods Cemetery.

Vermont Cemetery is located on Naperville's far south side, at 91st Street and Normantown Road. It is small and fenced in, closed to the public. There are graves in it from as early as the late 1700s. The other is Big Woods Cemetery, located just south of the intersection of Butterfield and Eola Roads. This cemetery is also quite small and is found behind the Big Woods church.

Perhaps the most surprising cemetery fact is the realization that the northeast corner of Benton and Washington Streets, in downtown Naperville, was at one time a pioneer cemetery! The elevated ground, with the vintage-house-turned-offices building certainly gives no indication of the former use of the land! Kailer Monuments Works also operated from this location, in 1871.

HauntedNaperville.com

A former Cemetery at Washington and Benton Streets

The cemetery at the corner of Benton and Washington apparently was quite crowded, and this overcrowding was one of the reasons Naperville businessman George Martin felt the need for an "official community cemetery." So, in March of 1843, the kind George Martin donated two acres of land along Washington Street to be used as Naperville's community cemetery. In 1850, it became the Naperville Cemetery. It is still in use today.

But get this: In 1843, a man was paid $52, by the city of Naperville, to *move all the graves* from the Benton Street Cemetery over to the new Naperville Cemetery down the street! Unfortunately, the task proved too overwhelming and grisly and the project was abandoned half way through! That means "pieces of grandma" are in two different cemeteries! *--No wonder these cemeteries so haunted!* A dead person won't rest well if he's buried in multiple places at the same time...

The building pictured above - that stands on the corner today - was at one time the home of Maureen Collins Crummy. In the summer of 1946, Ms. Crummy was having remodeling work done on the house. The remodeling required a bit of excavation... bad idea when the home is built on a former cemetery! It didn't take long for the workmen to begin hitting buried tombstones on the property! Some of the stones dated back to 1862!

In 1846, realizing the need for a Catholic burial ground, the parish of Saints Peter and Paul Church purchased an acre of land on Columbia Street and opened the Saints Peter and Paul Cemetery, still in use today. Originally it was primarily a German burial place.

In 1920, The Naperville Cemetery Association purchased an additional 15 acres to the west of the two-acre Naperville Cemetery bringing the cemetery to its current size.

The Streets of Naperville

Naperville's First Halloween Party?

Our town's most successful undertaker, Arthur Beidelman, threw the first known Halloween party in Naperville back in October of 1911.

At the time, Beidelman owned a tombstone/monument service at 318 S. Washington, just south of Chicago Avenue on Washington. The address doesn't exist today, but the location would be at approximately where the alley is just north of the park.

Arthur's business was in a building set back from Washington Street behind the home of Joe Koehly. The home's street location later became the Ackman Funeral Home.

In that back building, Art Beidelman threw what appears to be Naperville's first Halloween party. The children came from all over Naperville to participate. All kinds of amusements were available including fortune telling, and Hide and Seek amongst actual tombstones, vaults, and coffins!

According to the reports, the children relished the opportunity to play tricks and get treats while donning the garb of, (this is a quote from the newspaper story) "ghosts, witches, Indians, fairies and Negroes." A European lunch was served in the Beidelman living quarters upstairs.

The Witches Waddle

On October 3rd, 1943, Naperville High School, then located on Washington Street near Spring Avenue, hosted a Halloween party they called "The Witches Waddle Party!"

It appeared to be a somewhat reserved affair with music, dancing, ping-pong, and checkers! There was one event in the evening festivities that put a Halloween scare into just about everybody: there was a haunted ghost walk in the dark during which Shorty Watts pretended to be a corpse rising from his coffin. Evidently it was *pretty creepy...*

The evening ended with punch & cookies.

But before you go writing Naperville's youth off as "Halloween Softies," know this: on the same evening as the Witches Waddle Party, Naperville Halloween hoodlums, on the other side of town, took their toll on the city by lighting hundreds of fires in area leaf piles, as well as breaking *over 90 street lamps*!

Happy Halloween....

HauntedNaperville.com

In Closing...

Like a sun that sets and brings closure to another day, so too, this page brings closure to our final chapter. I hope you have enjoyed the journey.

Until next time,

Kev

HauntedNaperville.com

HauntedNaperville.com

Kevin is an award-winning public speaker and is available to speak to your group, organization, or church.

Call 630.205.2664
for more Information.

HauntedNaperville.com

Kevin's new book:

The Grave Robber Next Door... *A Love Story*

Now, for the first, the true story of Naperville's Infamous Grave Robber, from 1912, is being told... *Available Now.*

Notes

HauntedNaperville.com

Made in the USA
Charleston, SC
19 October 2015